Maigret and the Bum

Georges Simenon

Maigret and
the Bum

Translated by from the French by Jean Stewart

A Harvest Book • Harcourt, Inc.

A Helen and Kurt Wolff Book

Orlando   Austin   New York   San Diego   Toronto   London www.HarcourtBooks.com

Originally published in French under the title *Maigret et le clochard*.

Maigret is a registered trademark of the Estate of Georges Simenon.

Library of Congress Cataloging-in-Publication Data
Simenon, Georges, 1903–1989.
Maigret and the bum.
"A Helen and Kurt Wolff book."
Translation of Maigret et le clochard.
I. Title.
PZ3.S5892Maega [PQ2637. I53] 843′.9′12 73-9850
ISBN 0-15-602839-5

Printed in the United States of America
First Harvest edition 1982

A C E G I J H F D B

Maigret and the Bum

youth · brightness · joviality

For a moment, somewhere between the Quai des Orfèvres and the Pont Marie, Maigret halted, so briefly that Lapointe, who was walking beside him, did not notice. And yet, during the space of a few seconds, perhaps for less than a second, the superintendent had become a young man again, no older than his companion.

It was probably due to the quality of the air, the brightness, the smell, the taste of it. There had been a morning just like this, other mornings like it, when as a young detective newly appointed to the Police Judiciaire, which Parisians still called the Sûreté, Maigret had belonged to the Public Highways Squad and had walked the streets of Paris from morning till night.

Although it was March 25, this was the first real spring day, especially clear after a last heavy shower that had fallen during the night, accompanied by the distant rumble of thunder. For the first time that year, too, Maigret had left his overcoat hanging in the closet of his office, and from time to time the breeze blew open his unbuttoned jacket.

Because of that breath from the past, he had unconsciously begun to walk at his old pace, neither fast nor

3

slow, not exactly the pace of an idler pausing to watch trivial incidents in the street, nor yet that of a man making for a definite goal.

His hands clasped behind his back, he looked about him, to right and left and into the air, mentally recording visual images to which he had long ceased to pay attention.

For so short a journey, there had been no point in taking one of the black cars lined up in the courtyard of police headquarters, and the two men walked along the embankment. As they crossed the square in front of Notre Dame, a flight of pigeons took off; a big yellow coach, come from Cologne, had already brought the first party of tourists.

Crossing the iron footbridge, they had reached the Ile Saint-Louis, and at one of the windows Maigret had noticed a young housemaid in uniform and muslin cap, looking like a character out of a boulevard comedy. A butcher's boy, also in uniform, was delivering meat a little farther on; a postman was leaving an apartment building.

Buds had burst open that very morning, and the trees were speckled with pale green.

"The Seine's still high," observed Lapointe, who had not spoken until now.

It was true. For the past month the rain had barely stopped for more than a few hours at a time, and almost every evening the television showed rivers overflowing their banks, towns and villages with water pouring through their streets. The Seine was a yellowish flood, carrying along refuse, broken boxes, branches of trees.

The two men walked along the Quai de Bourbon as

4

far as the Pont Marie, and as they crossed the bridge at the same leisurely pace, they could see downstream a grayish-colored barge with the red and white triangle of the Compagnie Générale painted on her bow. Her name was *Le Poitou,* and a crane, whose grunting and creaking mingled with the confused noises of the city, was unloading the sand with which her holds were full.

Another barge was moored above the bridge, some fifty yards upstream from the first. She was cleaner-looking, as if she had been polished that very morning, and a Belgian flag was fluttering lazily over her stern, while, close to the white cabin, a baby lay asleep cradled in a canvas hammock, and a tall man with pale blond hair was looking out expectantly toward the riverbank.

The boat's name, in gilt letters, was *De Zwarte Zwaan,* a Flemish name that meant nothing to either Maigret or Lapointe.

It was two or three minutes to ten. The policemen reached the Quai des Célestins, and as they were about to go down the ramp toward the port a car stopped and three men got out, slamming the door behind them.

"Hullo! That's well timed. . . ."

They had come from the Palais de Justice, too, but from the more imposing part of it reserved for magistrates. There was Parrain, the deputy public prosecutor, Dantziger, the examining magistrate, and an old clerk of the court whose name Maigret could never remember, although he had met him hundreds of times.

Passers-by on their way to work, children playing on the pavement opposite did not suspect that a police investigation was under way. In the clear morning light, there was nothing impressive about it. The deputy public prose-

5

cutor pulled a gold cigarette case from his pocket and automatically offered it to Maigret, who had his pipe in his mouth.

"Of course . . . I was forgetting. . . ."

He was tall and slender, fair-haired and distinguished-looking, and the superintendent reflected, not for the first time, that this was typical of the public prosecutor's department. Dantziger, the examining magistrate, was short and tubby and casually dressed. There are all sorts of examining magistrates. Why were the people in the prosecutor's office always as elegant, as polite, and often as haughty as the private secretaries of cabinet ministers?

"Shall we go, messieurs?"

They went down the unevenly paved ramp as far as the water's edge, not far from the barge.

"Is that the one?"

Maigret knew no more about it than his companions. He had read the brief newspaper reports of what had happened during the night, and a telephone call half an hour previously had asked him to be present at the investigation by the office of the public prosecutor.

He was quite glad to do so. He was back among people and in an atmosphere with which he was not unfamiliar. The five men walked together toward the motor barge, while the tall blond bargeman set out to meet them along the plank that connected it with the bank.

"Take my hand," he said to the deputy public prosecutor, who was walking in front. "It'll be safer, *n'est-ce pas?*"

He had a pronounced Flemish accent. His strongly marked features, his pale eyes, his long arms and his way of moving recalled those Belgian racing cyclists whom one sees being interviewed after an event.

The noise of the crane unloading sand could be heard even more loudly here.

"Your name is Josef van Houtte?" Maigret asked, after glancing at a piece of paper.

"Jef van Houtte, yes, monsieur."

"Are you the owner of this boat?"

"Of course I'm the owner of it, monsieur. Who else could be?"

A good smell of cooking rose from the cabin, and at the foot of the stairs, which were covered with floral-patterned linoleum, a young woman could be seen coming and going.

Maigret pointed to the baby lying in its cradle.

"Is that your son?"

"That's not a son, monsieur, that's a daughter. Yolande, her name is. My sister's called Yolande, too, and she's it's godmother. . . ."

Parrain, the deputy public prosecutor, felt impelled to intervene, after motioning to the clerk to take notes.

"Tell us what happened."

"Well! I fished him out and the chap on the other boat helped me. . . ."

He pointed to the *Poitou,* at the stern of which a man, leaning against the tiller, was looking at them as if waiting for his turn.

A tug hooted repeatedly and sailed slowly past, going

upstream with four barges behind it. Each time one of them drew level with the *Zwarte Zwaan*, Jef van Houtte raised his right arm in greeting.

"Did you know the drowned man?"

"I'd never set eyes on him before. . . ."

"How long have you been berthed at this quay?"

"Since last night. I've come from Jeumont with a cargo of slates for Rouen. . . . I meant to pass through Paris and stop for the night at the Suresnes lock . . . I suddenly noticed that something was wrong with the engine . . . Us lot aren't keen on sleeping in the middle of Paris, you understand?"

From a distance, Maigret caught sight of two or three down-and-outs sitting about under the bridge, including a very stout woman whom he fancied he had seen before.

"How did it happen? Did the man jump into the water?"

"I don't think so, you know, monsieur. If he'd jumped into the water, what would the other two have been doing here?"

"What time was it? Where were you? Tell us everything that happened during the evening. You had moored by the quay shortly before nightfall?"

"That's right."

"Did you notice a bum under the bridge?"

"That's not the sort of thing one notices. There's nearly always some of them."

"What did you do next?"

"We had our supper, Hubert and Anneke and me. . . ."

"Who's Hubert?"

"He's my brother. He works with me. Anneke's my wife. Her name's Anna but we call her Anneke. . . ."

"And then?"

"My brother put on his good suit and went to a dance. He's the age for that, isn't he?"

"How old is he?"

"Twenty-two."

"Is he here?"

"He's gone shopping. He'll be back."

"What did you do after supper?"

"I went to work on the engine. I saw straight away that there was an oil leak, and as I wanted to set off this morning, I began to mend it."

He was casting watchful glances at them each in turn, with the mistrustful air of people who are unused to dealing with the law.

"When did you finish the job?"

"I didn't finish it, not until this morning."

"Where were you when you heard cries?"

He scratched his head, staring at the great gleaming spotless deck.

"First I went up once to smoke a cigarette and see if Anneke was asleep."

"What time was that?"

"About ten o'clock . . . I don't know exactly. . . ."

"Was she asleep?"

"Yes, monsieur. And the baby was asleep, too. Some nights she cries, because she's cutting her first teeth. . . ."

"Did you go back to your engine?"

"Of course . . ."

"Was it dark in the cabin?"

"Yes, monsieur, because my wife was asleep."

"And on deck, too?"

"Sure."

"And then?"

"Then, a long time after, I heard the noise of an engine, as if a car was stopping not far from the boat."

"Didn't you go and find out?"

"No, monsieur. Why should I have?"

"Go on."

"A little later, there was a splash. . . ."

"As if someone was falling into the Seine?"

"Yes, monsieur."

"And then?"

"I went up the ladder and stuck my head through the hatchway."

"What did you see?"

"Two men running toward the car . . ."

"So there really was a car?"

"Yes, monsieur. A red car. A Peugeot 403."

"Was it light enough for you to make it out?"

"There's a street lamp just above the wall."

"What were the two men like?"

"One was a short man in a light-colored raincoat, and he had broad shoulders."

"And the other?"

"I didn't see him so clearly because he got into the car first. He started up the engine immediately. . . ."

"You didn't notice the registration number?"

"The what?"

"The number on the license plate?"

"I only know there were two nines, and it ended in seventy-five. . . ."

"When did you hear the shouts?"

"When the car started off . . ."

"In other words, there was an interval between the time when the man was thrown into the water and the moment when he called out? Otherwise you'd have heard the shouts earlier?"

"I guess so, monsieur. At night it's quieter than now."

"What time was it?"

"After midnight . . ."

"Were there any people on the bridge?"

"I didn't look up. . . ."

On the embankment, beyond the wall, some passers-by had stopped, their curiosity aroused by the sight of these men arguing on the deck of a barge. It struck Maigret that the vagrants had moved several yards nearer. Meanwhile, the crane kept on scooping up sand from the hold of the *Poitou* and emptying it into trucks that stood waiting for their turn.

"Did he call out loudly?"

"Yes, monsieur . . ."

"What sort of a shout was it? Was he calling for help?"

"He shouted. . . . Then there was nothing more to be heard. . . . Then . . ."

"What did you do?"

"I jumped into the punt and unfastened it. . . ."

"Could you see the drowning man?"

"No, monsieur . . . Not right away . . . The skipper of the *Poitou* must have heard, too, for he was running the whole length of his craft trying to catch hold of something with his boat hook. . . ."

"Carry on . . ."

The Fleming seemed to be doing his best, but he found it hard, and beads of sweat appeared on his forehead.

"He was saying, 'There! . . . There! . . .' "

"Who was?"

"The skipper of the *Poitou*."

"And could you see?"

"Sometimes I could see, other times I couldn't."

"Because the body was sinking?"

"Yes, monsieur . . . And it was being carried away by the current. . . ."

"Your punt was, too, I suppose?"

"Yes, monsieur . . . The other man jumped into it. . . ."

"The man from the *Poitou?*"

Jef gave a sigh, probably reflecting that his interlocutors were not very bright. The whole thing was quite straightforward to him, and he must have been through similar scenes more than once in his life.

"Between you, you fished him out?"

"Yes . . ."

"What state was he in?"

"His eyes were still open, and when he was in the boat he was sick. . . ."

"He didn't say anything?"

"No, monsieur."

"Did he seem frightened?"

"No, monsieur."

"What did he seem like?"

"Nothing in particular. He stopped moving at last, and the water went on running out of his mouth."

"Were his eyes still open?"

"Yes, monsieur. I thought he was dead."

"Did you go for help?"

"No, monsieur. It wasn't me."

"Was it your mate from the *Poitou?*"

"No. Somebody shouted to us from off the bridge."

"So there was someone on the Pont Marie?"

"By then there was. He asked us if somebody had been drowned. I said yes. He shouted that he would go and tell the police."

"Did he do so?"

"He must have, for not long after a couple of cops came up on bikes."

"Was it raining already?"

"It started raining and thundering when we'd hoisted the man onto the deck."

"Of your barge?"

"Yes . . ."

"Did your wife wake up?"

"The light was on in the cabin, and Anneke had put on her coat and was watching us."

"When did you see the blood?"

"When we'd laid the man down beside the tiller. It was pouring out of a crack he'd got in his head."

"A crack?"

"A hole . . . I don't know what you'd call it. . . ."

"Did the policemen arrive immediately?"

"Almost immediately."

"And the passer-by who'd informed them?"

"I didn't see him again."

"You don't know who it was?"

"No, monsieur."

In the morning light it required some effort to imagine that midnight scene, which Jef van Houtte was describing as best he could, groping for his words as if he had to translate them one by one from Flemish.

"I suppose you know that the bum had been knocked on the head before being thrown into the water?"

"That's what the doctor said. Because one of the cops went to fetch a doctor. Then an ambulance came. Once they'd taken away the man's body, I had to swab the deck, where there was a great pool of blood. . . ."

"What happened, in your opinion?"

"I couldn't say, monsieur."

"You told the policemen . . ."

"I told them what I believed, didn't I?"

"Tell me again."

"I suppose he'd been sleeping under the bridge. . . ."

"But you hadn't seen him before?"

"I hadn't taken any notice. . . . There's always people sleeping under the bridges. . . ."

"All right. Then a car drove down the ramp. . . ."

"A red car . . . that I'm sure of. . . ."

"It stopped not far from your barge?"

He nodded and flung out his arm toward a certain point on the riverbank.

"Did the engine keep on running?"

This time he shook his head.

"But you heard footsteps?"

"Yes, monsieur."

"Two people's footsteps?"

"I saw two men coming back toward the car. . . ."

"You didn't see them go toward the bridge?"

"I was working down below, on the engine."

"Might these two men, one of whom was wearing a light-colored raincoat, have knocked out the vagrant as he lay asleep and then thrown him into the Seine?"

"When I went up, he was in the water already. . . ."

"The doctor's report states that he could not have received that injury to his head while falling into the water. . . . Not even if he had accidentally fallen on the edge of the quay . . ."

Van Houtte stared at them as if to say that it was none of his business.

"Can we question your wife?"

"I don't mind your talking to Anneke. Only she won't understand you, for she speaks only Flemish. . . ."

The deputy public prosecutor glanced at Maigret as if to ask him whether he had any questions to put, and the superintendent shook his head. If he had any, they would come later, when the gentlemen from the public prosecutor's office had gone away.

"When shall we be able to leave?" the bargeman asked.

"As soon as you've signed your statement. On condition you let us know where you are going . . ."

"To Rouen."

"You'll have to keep us informed of your subsequent movements. My clerk will bring you the documents to sign."

"When?"

"Probably in the early afternoon . . ."

This clearly annoyed the bargeman.

"By the way, what time did your brother come back on board?"

"Soon after the ambulance had left."

"Thank you . . ."

Once again Jef van Houtte helped him across the narrow gangway, and the little party made its way toward the bridge, while the down-and-outs withdrew a few yards.

"What d'you think about it, Maigret?"

"I think it's odd. It's pretty uncommon for a down-and-out to be attacked."

Under the arch of the Pont Marie, up against the stone wall, a kind of nook had been contrived. It was shapeless and nameless, and yet it had apparently provided for some time past a resting place for a human being.

The stupefaction of the deputy public prosecutor was comical to behold, and Maigret could not help telling him:

"There are places like that under all the bridges. In fact, you can see a shelter of this sort just opposite police headquarters."

"And the police do nothing about it?"

"If we demolish them, they spring up again a little farther off. . . ."

It was made of old boxes and pieces of tarpaulin. There was just enough room there for a man to lie curled up. The ground was covered with straw, torn blankets, and newspapers, which exuded a strong smell in spite of the draft under the bridge.

The deputy public prosecutor carefully avoided touching anything, and it was Maigret who bent down to make a rapid inventory.

An iron cylinder with holes and a grill had served as a stove and was still covered with whitish ash. Beside it lay pieces of charcoal, picked up heaven knows where. Turning over the blankets, the superintendent uncovered a secret hoard: two hunks of stale bread, a few inches of garlic sausage, and, in another corner, some books, whose titles he read out in an undertone.

"Verlaine's *Sagesse* . . . Bossuet's *Oraisons Funèbres* . . ."

He picked up a journal that must have been lying about in the rain for a long time and that had probably been extracted from someone's garbage heap. It was an old number of *La Presse Médicale*. . . .

Finally, part of a book, the second half of Las Cases's *Memorial de Sainte-Hélène*.

Dantziger, the magistrate, seemed just as stupefied as the man from the office of the public prosecutor.

"Funny sort of things he read," he commented.

"I don't suppose he had much choice. . . ."

Still looking under the tattered blankets, Maigret discovered some garments: a much-patched gray sweater with paint stains on it, which had presumably belonged to a painter, a pair of yellowish twill trousers, some felt slippers with worn-out soles, and five odd socks. Finally, a pair of scissors with one of the points broken.

"Is the man dead?" inquired Deputy Public Prosecutor Parrain, keeping at a safe distance for fear of catching fleas.

17

"He was alive an hour ago, when I rang up the Hôtel Dieu."

"Are they hoping to save him?"

"They're trying to. . . . He's got a fractured skull, and, furthermore, they're afraid of pneumonia developing. . . ."

Maigret was fingering a dilapidated baby carriage that the man must have used when he went rummaging in garbage piles. Turning toward the little group of watchful onlookers, he scanned their faces each in turn. Some of them looked away. Others expressed nothing but bewilderment.

"Come here, you! . . ." he told the woman, beckoning to her.

If it had happened thirty years earlier, when he was working on the Public Highways Squad, he could have put a name to each face, for at that period he had known most of the down-and-outs in Paris.

They had not altered much, in fact, but they had become far fewer.

"Where d'you sleep?"

The woman smiled at him ingratiatingly.

"Over there . . ." she said, pointing to the Pont Louis-Philippe.

"Did you know the man they fished out last night?"

She had a puffy face and her breath smelled of sour wine. She stood with her hands on her stomach, nodding her head.

"We used to call him Doc."

"Why?"

"Because he was an educated sort of man. . . . They say he really used to be a doctor once. . . ."

"Had he been living under the bridges a long time?"

"Years . . ."

"How many?"

"I don't know . . . I've stopped counting them. . . ."

This made her laugh, and she tossed back a lock of gray hair that hung over her face. When her mouth was shut, she looked about sixty. But when she spoke she disclosed an almost toothless jaw, and she seemed much older. There was still a twinkle in her eyes, however. From time to time she turned toward the others as though calling them to witness.

"It's true, isn't it?" she asked them.

They nodded, although ill at ease in the presence of the law and these overdressed gentlemen.

"Did he live alone?"

That made her laugh afresh.

"Who'd he have lived with?"

"Has he always lived under this bridge?"

"Not always . . . I used to know him under the Pont-Neuf . . . and before that in the Quai de Bercy. . . ."

"Did he go to the Halles?"

For that was where most down-and-outs forgathered at night.

"No," she replied.

"Did he forage in garbage heaps?"

"Sometimes . . ."

In spite of the baby carriage, therefore, he could not have been a collector of old papers and rags, and this would account for his already being in bed at nightfall.

"He was mostly a sandwich man. . . ."

"What else do you know?"

"Nothing . . ."

19

"Did he never talk to you?"

"Of course he did . . . In fact, it was me that used to cut his hair now and then. . . . Folks must help one another. . . ."

"Did he drink much?"

Maigret knew that the question was meaningless, since practically all of them drank.

"Red wine?"

"Like we all do."

"A lot?"

"I've never seen him sozzled. . . . Not like me . . ."

And she began laughing again.

"I know you, you know, and I know you're not a bad sort. You had me up for questioning once in your office, a long time ago, twenty years ago maybe, when I was still on the job at the Porte Saint-Denis. . . ."

"Did you hear nothing last night?"

She flung out her arm to point at the Pont Louis-Philippe, as though to show what a distance it was from the Pont Marie.

"It's too far off. . . ."

"You saw nothing?"

"Only the headlights of the ambulance. . . . I came a little closer, not too close for fear of being picked up, and I recognized it was an ambulance. . . ."

"And the rest of you?" Maigret asked the three down-and-outs.

They shook their heads, still ill at ease.

"Suppose we went to see the skipper of the *Poitou?*" suggested the deputy public prosecutor, who felt uncomfortable in these surroundings.

The man was expecting them. He was very unlike the

Fleming. He, too, had his wife and children on board, but the barge did not belong to him, and it almost always did the same journey, between the sand pits of the upper Seine and Paris. His name was Justin Goulet; he was forty-five. He was short and squat, with shrewd eyes, and an unlit cigarette clung to the corner of his lips.

Here, they had to speak loudly because of the noise from the nearby crane, which went on unloading sand.

"It's queer, isn't it?"

"What's queer?"

"That people should bother to do in a bum and chuck him in the water. . . ."

"Did you see them?"

"I didn't see anything at all."

"Where were you?"

"When they beat up the fellow? In my bunk . . ."

"What did you hear?"

"I heard somebody yelling. . . ."

"No car?"

"I may have heard a car, but there are cars going by all the time up there on the embankment and I didn't pay attention. . . ."

"Did you go up on deck?"

"In pajamas . . . I didn't waste time putting on my trousers. . . ."

"And your wife?"

"She said in her sleep, 'Where are you going?' "

"Once you were on deck what did you see?"

"Nothing . . . the Seine flowing by as usual, with eddies . . . I shouted 'Ahoy!' so that the man might answer and so's I could find out whereabouts he was. . . ."

"Where was Jef van Houtte at this point?"

"The Fleming?. . . I finally caught sight of him on the deck of his barge. . . . He started to unfasten his punt. . . . When the stream brought him level with me, I jumped in. . . . The man in the water kept surfacing and then disappearing again. . . . The Fleming tried to catch him with my boat hook. . . ."

"A boat hook with a big iron hook at the end?"

"They're all like that. . . ."

"Couldn't he have incurred that injury to his head when you were trying to catch hold of him?"

"Surely not. . . . In the end we got him by the seat of his trousers. . . . I leaned over at once and caught him by one leg. . . ."

"Had he fainted?"

"His eyes were open."

"Did he say nothing?"

"He vomited up some water. . . . Afterwards, on the Fleming's boat, we saw that he was bleeding. . . ."

"I think that's all," muttered the deputy public prosecutor, who seemed to find the story rather tedious.

"I'll look after the rest," Maigret replied.

"Are you going to the hospital?"

"I'll go there presently. The doctors say it'll be several hours before he's in a fit state to speak. . . ."

"Keep me informed. . . ."

"I certainly will. . . ."

As they went back under the Pont Marie, Maigret said to Lapointe:

"Go and ring up the district police station and ask them to send me an officer."

"Where shall I find you, Chief?"

"Here . . ."

And he solemnly shook hands with the people from the department of public prosecution.

A re those judges?" asked the fat woman as she watched the three men walking away.

"They're magistrates," Maigret corrected her.

"It's the same thing, isn't it?"

And, after giving a faint whistle: "They're taking as much trouble as if he'd been one of the nobs, aren't they? Was he a real doctor, then?"

Maigret did not know. He seemed in no hurry to find out. He was living in the present, with a persistent sense of having experienced these things before, a long time ago. Lapointe had disappeared at the top of the ramp. The deputy public prosecutor, flanked by the little magistrate and the clerk, was picking his steps carefully for fear of soiling his shoes.

Black and white in the sunshine, the *Zwarte Zwaan* was as spotless outside as its kitchen must have been. The tall Fleming, standing beside the steering wheel, was looking in his direction, and a small, slender woman, a real child-wife with hair so fair as to be almost white, was bending over the cradle, changing the child's diapers.

Despite the unceasing noise of the cars along the Quai des Célestins and of the crane unloading sand from the

Poitou, Maigret could hear birds singing and the lapping of the water.

The three down-and-outs still kept out of the way, and only the stout woman followed the superintendent under the bridge. Her blouse, which must once have been red, was now a faded pink.

"What's your name?"

"Léa. Big Léa, they call me. . . ."

This set her laughing, and her enormous breasts shook.

"Where were you last night?"

"I told you."

"Was there nobody with you?"

"Only Dédé, the smallest of them, over there with his back to you."

"Is he your friend?"

"They're all my friends."

"Do you always sleep under the same bridge?"

"I sometimes move around. . . . What are you looking for?"

For Maigret was once again bending over the queer collection of objects that constituted the worldly goods of the Doc. He felt more at ease now that the magistrates had left. He took his time and brought out from under the rags a frying pan, a mess tin, a spoon and fork.

Then he tried on a pair of glasses with steel rims, one lens of which was cracked, and everything became a blur.

"He only uses them for reading," explained the fat woman.

"What surprises me," he began, looking at her intently, "is not to find . . ."

She did not let him finish but moved a couple of yards

away, and from behind a big stone pulled out a liter bottle still half full of purplish wine.

"Have you drunk some of it?"

"Yes. I was going to finish it up. It won't be any good, after all, when the Doc comes back."

"When did you take it?"

"Last night, after the ambulance had taken him off."

"You've touched nothing else?"

She spat on the ground, with a solemn face. " I swear I haven't!"

He believed her. He knew from experience that the down-and-out do not rob one another. Indeed, it is unusual for them to rob anybody at all, not only because they would be spotted immediately but through a kind of indifference.

Across the river, on the Ile Saint-Louis, open windows revealed cozy apartments, and a woman could be seen brushing her hair at her dressing table.

"Do you know where he bought his wine?"

"I've seen him more than once coming out of a *bistrot* in Rue Ave-Maria. . . . It's quite close by . . . at the corner of Rue des Jardins. . . . "

"How did the Doc get on with the others?"

She thought hard, trying to please him.

"I couldn't really say. . . . He wasn't all that different. . . ."

"Did he never speak about his life?"

"None of us do. . . . Not without being really boozed up. . . ."

"Was he never boozed up?"

"Not really . . ."

Out of the pile of old newspapers that had served to keep the Doc warm, Maigret had just pulled out a small painted toy horse with one leg broken. He was not surprised to see it; neither was big Léa.

Someone came down the ramp with silent, springy steps, wearing rope-soled sandals, and headed for the Belgian barge. In each hand he carried a string bag full of provisions, from which protruded two long loaves and some fishes' tails.

This was undoubtedly the brother, for he was like a younger version of Jef van Houtte, with less pronounced features. He was wearing blue jeans and a white-striped jersey. Once on board the boat, he spoke to the other man, then glanced in Maigret's direction.

"Don't touch anything," said Maigret. "I may need you again. . . . If you should hear anything . . ."

"Can you see me turning up at your office, looking like this?"

That set her laughing again. Pointing to the bottle, she asked, "May I finish it off?"

He nodded, and went to meet Lapointe, who was now returning accompanied by a uniformed policeman. He gave the latter instructions: to watch over the heap of rubbish that constituted the Doc's fortune until the arrival of a specialist from the police records office.

After this, with Lapointe by his side, he made his way toward the *Zwarte Zwaan*.

"You are Hubert van Houtte?"

The youth, more taciturn or more suspicious than his brother, merely nodded.

"Did you go dancing last night?"

"Is there anything wrong about that?"

His accent was less pronounced. Maigret and Lapointe, standing on the bank, had to raise their heads to speak to him.

"What dance hall were you at?"

"Near Place de la Bastille . . . a narrow street where there are half a dozen of them. . . . This one was called Chez Léon. . . ."

"Did you know it already?"

"I'd been there a number of times. . . ."

"So you know nothing about what has happened?"

"Only what my brother told me. . . ."

Smoke was rising from a brass funnel on the deck. The woman had gone down into the cabin with her child, and from where they stood the superintendent and the inspector could smell cooking.

"When shall we be able to leave?"

"Probably this afternoon . . . as soon as the magistrate has got your brother to sign the statement. . . ."

Hubert van Houtte, clean-looking and well-groomed, had the same pink skin and pale blond hair as his brother.

A little later, Maigret and Lapointe crossed the Quai des Célestins, and at the corner of Rue de l'Ave-Maria they found a *bistrot* bearing the sign *Au Petit Turin*. The proprietor, in his shirt sleeves, was standing in the doorway. There was nobody inside.

"May we come in?"

He drew aside, astonished to see people like themselves entering his establishment. The place was minute, and apart from the counter there were only three tables for customers. The walls were painted apple green. From the ceiling there hung sausages, salami, and queer yellow cheeses shaped like bulging goatskin bottles.

"What can I bring you?"

"Some wine . . ."

"Chianti?"

Flasks in straw covers lined a whole shelf, but the proprietor filled their glasses from a bottle standing under the counter, meanwhile watching the two men with curiosity.

"Do you know a vagrant who's known as the Doc?"

"How is he? I hope he hasn't died?"

The Italian accent and the gesticulations of the proprietor contrasted with the Flemish accent and calm bearing of Jef van Houtte and his brother.

"You know what has happened?" Maigret asked.

"I know something happened to him last night."

"Who told you?"

"Another of the bums, this morning . . ."

"What were you told, exactly?"

"That there had been a to-do near the Pont Marie and that an ambulance had come to take away the Doc."

"Anything else?"

"Seems that the bargemen fished him out of the water. . . ."

"Did the Doc buy his wine from you?"

"Often . . ."

"Did he drink a lot?"

"About two liters a day . . . when he had the money . . ."

"How did he earn it?"

"Like they all do . . . odd jobs in the market or elsewhere . . . or walking the streets with advertisement boards. . . . I was always glad to let him have it on credit. . . ."

"Why?"

"Because he wasn't a no-good like the rest. . . . He saved my wife. . . ."

The woman was there in the kitchen, almost as stout as Léa but very alert.

"You're talking about me?"

"I was telling how the Doc . . ."

Then she came into the bar, wiping her hands on her apron. "Is it true that someone tried to kill him? . . . Are you from the police? . . . D'you think he's going to get over it?"

"We don't know yet," the superintendent replied evasively. "What did he do for you?"

"Well, if you'd seen me a couple of years ago, you wouldn't have recognized me. . . . I was covered with eczema, and my face was as red as a piece of meat on a butcher's slab. . . . It had been going on for months and months. . . . At the outpatients' clinic they tried out all sorts of treatments on me. They gave me ointments that smelled so horrible I was disgusted with myself. . . . Nothing did any good. I was hardly allowed to eat anything, and in any case I'd lost my appetite. . . . And they gave me injections. . . ."

The proprietor listened, nodding.

"One day when the Doc was sitting there, in that corner by the door, and I was complaining to the fruit and vegetable woman, I felt he was looking at me in an odd sort of

30

way.... A little later he said to me in the same tone of voice as though he'd been ordering a glass of wine:

"'I think I can cure you....'

"I asked him if he was really a doctor, and he smiled.

"'I've not been disqualified from practicing,' he said quietly."

"Did he give you a prescription?"

"No. He asked me for a little money, two hundred francs, if I remember rightly, and he went off himself to get some little packets of powder from the druggist.

"'Take one in warm water before each meal.... and wash yourself, morning and night, in salt water....'

"Believe it or not, two months after that my skin was all right again...."

"Did he attend anyone else besides you?"

"I don't know. He didn't talk much."

"Did he come here every day?"

"Practically every day, to buy his couple of liters...."

"Was he always by himself? Did you ever see him with anyone you didn't know?"

"No."

"Did he never tell you his real name, nor where he lived formerly?"

"I only know he had a daughter.... We've got one, who's at school now.... Once, when she was staring at him curiously, he said to her:

"'Don't be afraid of me.... I've got a little girl, too. ...'"

Lapointe was probably somewhat surprised to see Maigret attach so much importance to the story of this down-and-out. In the press it would have provided merely a few lines among the news items.

What Lapointe did not know, because he was too young, was that this was the first time in Maigret's career that a crime had been committed against one of the down-and-outs.

"How much do I owe you?"

"Won't you have one more? To drink the health of poor old Doc?"

They drank the second glass, for which the Italian refused to let them pay. Then they crossed over the Pont Marie. A few minutes later they went in under the gray archway of the Hôtel Dieu. Here they had a lengthy argument with a cantankerous woman on duty behind a window.

"You don't know his name?"

"Only that he's known on the embankment as the Doc and that he was brought here last night . . ."

"Last night I wasn't here. . . . Which department have they taken him to?"

"I don't know. . . . Just now I spoke on the telephone to an intern who said nothing about an operation. . . ."

"Do you know the name of the intern?"

"No."

She flicked over the pages of a register and made two or three telephone calls.

"What did you say your name was?"

"Superintendent Maigret . . ."

The name meant nothing to the woman, who repeated into the receiver:

"Superintendent Maigret . . ."

Finally, after about ten minutes, she sighed, as though granting them a favor:

"Take staircase C. . . . Go up to the third floor. . . . Ask for the sister in charge of that floor. . . ."

They met nurses, young doctors, patients in hospital uniform, and through open doors caught sight of rows of beds.

On the third floor they had to wait yet again, for the sister in charge was having an animated discussion with two men, whose request she appeared to be refusing.

"I can't do anything about it," she finally flung at them. "Speak to the head office. I don't make the rules."

They went off, muttering uncomplimentary remarks between their teeth, and she turned to Maigret.

"Is it you who've come about the vagrant?"

"Superintendent Maigret . . ." he repeated.

She was searching her memory. The name meant nothing to her, either. This was another world, a world of numbered wards, of separate departments, of beds lined up in huge rooms, each bed having at its foot a card inscribed with mysterious signs.

"How is he?"

"I believe Dr. Magnin is with him at this moment."

"Has he been operated on?"

"Who said anything to you about an operation?"

"I don't know . . . I thought . . ."

Maigret did not feel at home here, and it made him diffident.

"Under what name have you registered him?"

"The name on his identity card."

"Have you got the card?"

"I can show it to you."

She went into a small glass-paneled office at the end of the passage and promptly found a filthy identity card still damp from the water of the Seine.

Surname: Keller.

First names: François Marie Florentin.

Occupation: rag-and-bone man.

Birthplace: Mulhouse, Bas-Rhin.

According to this document, the man was sixty-three years old, and his address in Paris was a flophouse, in Place Maubert, which the superintendent knew quite well and which served as official residence for a number of vagrants.

"Has he recovered consciousness?"

She tried to take back the identity card, which the superintendent was putting in his pocket, and she grumbled:

"It's not in order . . . the regulations . . ,"

"Is Keller in a private ward?"

"Whatever next?"

"Take me to him. . . ."

She hesitated but eventually gave way.

"Well, you'll have to settle things with the doctor . . ."

Leading the way, she opened the third door, disclosing two rows of beds, all occupied. Most of the patients were lying down, and their eyes were open; two or three were standing about at the far end of the room, wearing hospital clothes, and chatting in low voices. Beside one of the beds, in the middle of the room, a dozen young men and women in white coats and caps stood round a short, broad-shouldered man with crew-cut hair, also clad in white, who appeared to be giving them a lecture.

"You can't disturb him just now. . . . You see he's busy. . . ."

However, she went up and whispered a few words in the ear of the doctor, who cast a glance in Maigret's direction and went on with his explanations.

"He'll have finished in a few minutes. He asks you to wait in his office. . . ."

She took them there. It was a small room with only a couple of chairs in it. On the desk stood a silver-framed photograph of a woman and three children with their heads close together.

Maigret hesitated, then emptied his pipe into the ash tray, which was crammed with cigarette butts, and filled himself another.

"Sorry to have kept you waiting, Superintendent. When Sister told me you were there, I was a bit surprised. . . . After all . . ."

Was he, too, going to say that, after all, the patient was merely a down-and-out? No.

". . . It's a straightforward business, I suppose?"

"I scarcely know anything about it yet and I'm counting on you to enlighten me. . . ."

"It's a fracture of the skull, a nice clean one, luckily, as my assistant must have told you over the phone this morning. . . ."

"They haven't X-rayed him yet. . . ."

"That's been done now. . . . He's got a good chance of pulling through, for the brain doesn't appear to be damaged. . . ."

"Could the fracture have been caused by a fall on the embankment?"

"Certainly not . . . The man had been struck a violent

blow with some heavy instrument such as a hammer, a monkey wrench, or a tire jack. . . ."

"Did it make him lose consciousness?"

"He lost consciousness to such an extent that he's still in a coma and may remain in it for several days. . . . Or, on the other hand, he might come round at any moment. . . ."

Maigret kept visualizing the riverbank, the Doc's shelter, the muddy water flowing a few yards away, and he recalled the remarks of the Flemish bargeman.

"Forgive me for persisting. . . . You say he'd had a blow on the head. . . . Only one?"

"Why do you ask that?"

"It might be important."

"At first glance I thought he might have received several blows. . . ."

"Why?"

"Because one ear is torn, and there are a number of superficial wounds on the face. Now that he's been shaved I've had a closer look. . . ."

"And your conclusion?"

"Where did it happen?"

"Under the Pont Marie."

"During a fight?"

"Apparently not. The man seems to have been lying asleep when he was attacked. . . . According to your observations, is that plausible?"

"Quite plausible."

"And do you think he lost consciousness immediately?"

"I'm practically sure of that. And after what you've

just told me, I can account for the torn ear and the scratches on the face. He was picked up out of the Seine, wasn't he? These minor injuries suggest that instead of being carried there he was dragged over the stones along the embankment. Is there any sand on that part of the embankment?"

"They're unloading sand from a barge a few yards away."

"I found traces of sand in the wounds."

"In your opinion, then, the Doc . . ."

"What did you say?" the doctor asked in some surprise.

"That's what they call him on the embankment. It's possible he may really have been a doctor."

And this was the first time, in thirty years, that Maigret had come across a doctor living under the bridges. He could remember finding there a former chemistry teacher from a provincial *lycée*, and a few years later a woman who had been a famous circus rider in her time.

"I'm convinced that he was lying down and probably asleep when his attacker, or attackers, struck him. . . ."

"Only one person must have struck him, since there was only a single blow. . . ."

"Quite true . . . He then lost consciousness, so that he must have appeared dead. . . ."

"That's very plausible."

"He was then dragged rather than carried to the edge of the Seine and tipped into the water. . . ."

The doctor was listening gravely, with a thoughtful look.

"Does that hold together?" Maigret persisted.

"Perfectly well."

"Is it medically possible that when he was in the river, being swept away by the current, he should have begun to scream?"

The professor scratched his head.

"You're asking a good deal of me, and I shouldn't like to give you a categorical answer. Let's say that I don't consider the thing impossible. On coming into contact with the cold water . . ."

"Would he have recovered consciousness, then?"

"Not necessarily. Patients in a coma sometimes speak and move about. . . . Let's assume . . ."

"Did he say nothing while you were examining him?"

"He gave an occasional moan."

"I was told that when he was picked out of the water his eyes were open. . . ."

"That proves nothing. I suppose you'd like to see him? Come with me."

He took them along to the third door, and the ward sister watched them pass in with some surprise and also no doubt with some disapproval.

The patients lying in their beds stared at the little party as it moved forward and came to a halt at one of the bedsides.

"There's not much to be seen. . . ."

Indeed, there was nothing to be seen but the bandages that surrounded the vagrant's face and head, revealing only his eyes, nose, and mouth.

"What are his chances of recovery?"

"Seventy per cent . . . Say eighty, for his heart's still strong. . . ."

"Thank you very much. . . ."

"You'll be informed as soon as he recovers consciousness. Leave your phone number with the ward sister. . . ."

It felt good to be outside again and to see the sun, the people in the street, a red and yellow coach unloading its tourists on the parvis of Notre Dame.

Once again, Maigret walked along in silence, his hands behind his back, and Lapointe, realizing that he was preoccupied, avoided speaking.

They went under the archway of police headquarters and climbed up the big staircase, which looked even dustier than usual in the sunlight, finally reaching the superintendent's office.

The first thing Maigret did was to fling the window wide open and look down at a string of barges drifting downstream.

"We'll have to send somebody from up there to look at his things. . . ."

"Up there" meant the police records office, with its technicians and specialists.

"The best thing would be to take the van and remove the whole lot."

He had no fear of other vagrants seizing the Doc's few belongings, but he was afraid, rather, of thieving urchins.

"Will you go to the Highways Department, meanwhile? . . . There can't be all that number of red 403's in Paris. Make a note of all the numbers that include two nines. Get help from as many men as you need to check up on the owners. . . ."

"Right, Chief . . ."

Once he was alone, Maigret set out his pipes and looked through the official correspondence piled up on his desk. Because of the fine weather, he wondered whether to lunch at the Brasserie Dauphine and finally decided to go home.

At this time of day the dining room was flooded with sunlight. Madame Maigret was wearing a dress with pink flowers, and it reminded him of Big Léa's blouse, which was almost the same pink.

He was deep in thought as he ate his *foie de veau en papillotes,* and his wife asked him:

"What are you thinking about?"

"About my tramp."

"What tramp?"

"A fellow who may once have been a doctor . . ."

"What has he done?"

"Nothing, as far as I know. But he nearly got his head split open while he was asleep under the Pont Marie. And then he was thrown into the water. . . ."

"Did he die?"

"Some bargeman fished him out in time. . . ."

"Why had somebody got it in for him?"

"That's what I'm wondering. . . . As it happens, he comes from the same part of the world as your brother-in-law."

Madame Maigret's sister lived in Mulhouse with her husband, a civil engineer. The Maigrets had been to visit her quite often.

"What's his name?"

"Keller . . . François Keller . . ."

"It's funny, but the name seems to ring a bell. . . ."

"It's a fairly common name in those parts. . . ."

"Suppose I called my sister?"

He shrugged his shoulders. Why not? He did not put much faith in it, but it would give his wife pleasure.

As soon as she had served coffee, she called Mulhouse; she had only a few minutes to wait for the connection, and during that time she kept saying to herself, as though trying to recollect:

"Keller . . . François Keller . . ."

The telephone rang.

"Hullo! . . . Hullo, yes! . . . Yes, mademoiselle, I asked for Mulhouse. . . . Is that you, Florence? . . . What d'you say? . . . Yes, it's me. . . . Why, no, nothing's the matter. . . . From Paris . . . I'm at home. . . . He's right beside me, drinking his coffee. . . . He's fine. . . . Everything's fine. . . . Yes, it is here too. . . . Spring at last . . .

"How are the children? . . . Flu? I had it last week. . . . Not badly . . . Listen . . . That's not what I'm calling you about. . . . Do you by any chance remember somebody called Keller? . . . François Keller? . . . What's that? . . . I'll ask him . . ."

And turning to Maigret, she inquired:

"How old is he?"

"Sixty-four."

"Sixty-four . . . Yes . . . You didn't know him personally? What's that you said? . . . Don't disconnect us, mademoiselle . . . Hullo! . . . Yes, he was a doctor. . . . For the past half-hour I've been trying to remember who had told me about him. . . . D'you think it was your husband?

"Yes... wait... I'm going to repeat what you've said to *my* husband, who seems to be getting impatient.... He married the Mervilles' daughter. Who are these Mervilles?... An Appeal Court judge?... He married the daughter of an Appeal Court judge?... Right... The father died... a long time ago... Right... Don't be surprised if I repeat everything, but otherwise I'd be afraid of forgetting something.... An old Mulhouse family... The grandfather had been mayor and... I can't hear you very well... his statue... I don't think that's very important.... It doesn't matter if you're not sure....

"Hullo!... So Keller married her... their only daughter... Rue du Sauvage?... The couple lived on Rue du Sauvage?... An eccentric?... Why?... You don't exactly know.... Oh, yes, I get your point ... a bit of a savage himself..."

She glanced at Maigret as though to say she was doing her utmost.

"Yes... yes... It doesn't matter if it's not interesting.... Where he's concerned, you never know.... Sometimes a detail that may seem quite unimportant ... Yes... In which year?... About twenty years ago, then... She was left some money by an aunt.... And he went away.... Not immediately... He still lived with her for a year or so....

"Had they any children?... One daughter?... Who?... Rousselet, pharmaceutical products?... Does she live in Paris?..."

She repeated, for her husband's benefit:

"They had a daughter who married young Rousselet of the pharmaceutical products firm, living in Paris...."

She returned to the telephone:

"I understand ... Listen ... Try to find out some more.... Yes ... Many thanks ... Love to your husband and the children. Call me back any time.... I'm not going out...."

There followed the sound of kisses. Now she spoke to Maigret:

"I was sure I knew the name. Did you understand? It seems as if it really was the same François Keller, who was a doctor and who married the daughter of a magistrate.... Her father died shortly before the marriage...."

"And the mother?" he inquired.

She looked at him sharply, wondering whether he was speaking ironically. "I don't know. Florence said nothing about her.... About twenty years ago Madame Keller inherited some money from one of her aunts. She's a very rich woman now.... The doctor was an eccentric.... You heard what I said? A bit of a savage, as my sister put it ... They left their home and settled in a big house near the cathedral.... He stayed with her for one year more, and then all of a sudden he disappeared.

"Florence is going to call her friends, particularly the older ones, to get more information.... She's promised to call me back.... Does it interest you?"

"Everything interests me," he sighed, getting up from his armchair to fetch a fresh pipe from the rack.

"Do you think it'll involve a journey to Mulhouse?"

"I don't know yet."

"Would you take me along?"

They smiled at one another. The window was open. The sun streamed in on them and made them think of holidays.

"See you this evening . . . I'll make a note of everything she tells me . . . even if it makes you laugh at us both."

THREE

Young Lapointe was presumably scouring Paris for red 403's. Janvier was not at his desk in the inspectors' room, either, for he had been summoned to the nursing home, where he was now pacing the corridors, waiting for his wife to present him with a fourth child.

"Are you doing anything urgent, Lucas?"

"Nothing that can't wait, Chief."

"Come into my room for a minute."

It was to send him to the Hôtel Dieu to collect the Doc's belongings. Maigret had forgotten about this in the morning.

"They'll probably send you from one office to another and rebuff you with lord knows what rules and regulations. . . . You'd do well to provide yourself with a letter that'll impress them, with as many official stamps as possible. . . ."

"Who shall I get to sign it?"

"Sign it yourself. With them, it's only the stamps that count. . . . I'd also like to have this François Keller's fingerprints. Actually, it'll be simpler to call the head of the hospital. . . ."

A sparrow on the window sill was watching them both

bestirring themselves in what must have appeared to it as a human nest. With the utmost politeness, Maigret gave notice of Sergeant Lucas's forthcoming visit, and everything went off quite smoothly.

"You won't need a letter," he declared, hanging up the receiver. "They'll take you straight to the director, and he'll show you round himself."

Left alone, a little later, he was looking through the pages of the Paris telephone directory.

"Rousselet . . . Rousselet . . . Aline . . . Amédée . . . Arthur . . ."

There were scores of Rousselets, but he found one entry in heavy type: Laboratories René Rousselet.

The labs were in the fourteenth *arrondissement,* near the Porte d'Orleans. This particular Rousselet's private address was given immediately below: Boulevard Suchet, XVIe.

It was half past two. The weather was still just as radiant, after a flurry of wind that had raised the dust of the pavements and seemed to threaten a storm.

"Hullo! May I speak to Madame Rousselet, please?"

A woman's voice, low-pitched and pleasant, asked: "Who is speaking?"

"Superintendent Maigret, of the Judiciary Police."

There was a pause, then:

"Can you tell me what it's about?"

"It's a personal matter. . . ."

"I am Madame Rousselet."

"Were you born at Mulhouse and was your maiden name Keller?"

"Yes."

"I should like to talk to you as soon as possible. . . . May I call on you?"

"Have you bad news for me?"

"I only want some information."

"When would you like to come?"

"As soon as I can get to you."

He heard her say to somebody, presumably a child: "Let me talk, Jeannot . . ."

She was evidently surprised, intrigued, and uneasy.

"I'll expect you, Superintendent. . . . Our apartment is on the third floor. . . ."

That morning he had enjoyed the atmosphere of the *quais*, which brought back to his mind so many memories, particularly of the walks he had often taken with Madame Maigret, when they used to stroll along the Seine from one end of Paris to the other. He was equally appreciative of the peaceful tree-lined avenues and elegant houses of the wealthy districts to which he was now driven by Inspector Torrence in a small police car.

"Shall I come up with you, Chief?"

"I think better not."

The apartment house had a wrought-iron doorway lined with glass, and the entrance hall was of white marble; the roomy elevator rose silently, without a jar or a creak. He barely had time to press the bell when the door opened and a manservant in a white jacket relieved him of his hat.

"This way, please . . ."

There was a red ball lying in the entrance hall, and a doll on the carpet, and he caught sight of a nurse taking a little girl in white along the passage. Another door opened, leading into a small sitting room adjoining the large living room.

"Come in, Superintendent . . ."

Maigret had reckoned that she must be about thirty-five. She looked younger. She was dark-haired and wore a lightweight suit. Her eyes, which had the same mellow softness as her voice, looked at him questioningly, while the manservant closed the door.

"Do sit down . . . Ever since you called me I've been wondering . . ."

Instead of going straight to the heart of the matter, he asked automatically:

"You have several children?"

"I've got four . . . Eleven, nine, seven, and three . . ."

It was probably the first time a policeman had entered her home, and she kept her eyes fixed on him.

"I wondered at first whether anything had happened to my husband . . ."

"Is he in Paris?"

"Not at the moment. He's at a conference in Brussels, and I called him immediately. . . ."

"Do you remember your father well, Madame Rousselet?"

She seemed to relax slightly. There were flowers everywhere, and the trees of the Bois de Boulogne could be seen through the large windows.

"I remember him, yes . . . although . . ."

She seemed reluctant to go on.

"When was the last time you saw him?"

"It was a very long time ago. . . . I was thirteen."

"Were you still living in Mulhouse?"

"Yes . . . I came to Paris only after my marriage. . . ."

"Was it at Mulhouse that you met your husband?"

"At La Baule, where we used to go every year, Mother and I . . ."

Children could be heard shouting and sliding about in the hall.

"Excuse me a moment. . . ."

She closed the door behind her and said something in a low but forceful tone.

"I'm sorry about that. . . . They're not at school today, and I had promised to take them out. . . ."

"Would you recognize your father?"

"I suppose so. . . . Yes . . ."

He produced the Doc's identity card from his pocket. According to the date of issue, the photograph was some five years old. It had been taken by one of those automatic cameras that are to be found in big stores and stations, and even at police headquarters.

François Keller had not shaved for the occasion and had made no attempt to spruce himself up. His cheeks were covered with a two- or three-inch growth of beard, which he must have cut from time to time with scissors. His hair had begun to recede on his temples, and the expression in his eyes was blank and indifferent.

"Is that him?"

She held the document in an unsteady hand and bent down to see it better. She was evidently shortsighted.

"This is not how I remembered him, but I'm practically sure it's my father. . . ."

She bent down closer.

"With a magnifying glass, I might be able to . . . Wait, I'll fetch one. . . ."

She left the identity card on a small table, disappeared, and came back a few minutes later with a lens.

"He had a scar above his left eye, quite small but deep. . . . See . . . You can't make it out very well in this photograph, but I think it's there. . . . Look for yourself. . . ."

Maigret peered through the magnifying glass.

"I remember it so clearly, because it was on account of me that he hurt himself. . . . We were taking a walk in the countryside one Sunday. . . . It was very hot, and there were masses of poppies growing alongside a field of corn. . . .

"I wanted to go and pick some. There was a barbed-wire fence round the field. . . . I was about eight years old. . . . My father held the barbed wire apart to let me get through. . . . He held the lower wire down with his foot and he was bending forward. . . . It's funny that I can picture the scene so clearly, when I've forgotten so many other things. . . . His foot must have slipped, and the barbed wire sprang up suddenly and hit him in the face. . . .

"My mother was afraid his eye might have been hurt. . . . He was bleeding a lot. . . . We went to a farm to get water and something to dress the wound with. . . .

"He was left with the scar. . . ."

All the time she spoke, she was watching Maigret anxiously and seemed to be trying to put off the moment when he would tell her exactly why he had come.

"Has anything happened to him?"

"He was injured last night, on the head again, but the doctors don't think his life is in danger. . . ."

"Did it happen in Paris?"

"Yes . . . On the bank of the Seine . . . Whoever attacked him then threw him into the water. . . ."

He kept his eyes fixed on her, watching her reactions, and she made no attempt to avoid his scrutiny.

"Do you know how your father was living?"

"Not exactly . . ."

"What do you mean?"

"When he left us . . ."

"You were thirteen, you told me. . . . Do you remember his leaving?"

"No . . . One morning I didn't see him about the house, and as I expressed surprise my mother told me he had gone for a long journey. . . ."

"When did you learn where he was?"

"A few months later, Mother informed me that he was in Africa, in the wilds, looking after natives. . . ."

"Was it true?"

"I assume it was. . . . Later, in fact, people who had met him out there told us about him. . . . He was living in Gabon, at a station some hundreds of miles from Libreville. . . ."

"Did he stay there long?"

"For several years, at any rate . . . In Mulhouse, some people considered him a kind of saint. . . . Others . . ."

He waited. She seemed hesitant.

"Others called him reckless and crazy. . . ."

"And you?"

"I think Mother had resigned herself once and for all. . . ."

"How old is she now?"

"Fifty-four . . . No, fifty-five . . . I know now that he had left her a letter which she never showed me, in which he said that he would probably never come back and that he was ready to let her divorce him. . . ."

"And did she?"

"No. Mother's a very devout Catholic. . . ."

"Does your husband know about it?"

"Of course. We hid nothing from him. . . ."

"Were you unaware that your father had come back to Paris?"

Her eyelids fluttered briefly, and she was on the point of telling a lie; Maigret was convinced of it.

"Yes and no . . . I never saw him again myself. . . . We knew nothing for certain, Mother and I. . . . But somebody from Mulhouse told her about a sandwich man he had met on Boulevard Saint-Michel, who looked strangely like my father. . . . An old friend of Mother's, it was . . . Apparently when he spoke the name François the man gave a start, but afterward pretended not to have recognized him. . . ."

"Did it never occur to you or to your mother to approach the police?"

"What would have been the good? He had chosen his own way of life. He was probably not cut out to share ours. . . ."

"Did you never wonder about him?"

"We talked about him several times, my husband and I. . . ."

"And what about your mother?"

"I asked her various questions, of course, before and after I got married. . . ."

"What is her point of view?"

"It's hard to say, right away, in a few sentences. . . . She's sorry for him. . . . So am I . . . although I sometimes wonder if he isn't happier this way. . . ."

She added in a lower tone, with some embarrassment:

"There are some people who can't fit in with the kind of life we lead. And, besides, Mother . . ."

She rose, restlessly, went to the window and looked out for a moment before turning to face him again.

"I don't mean to blame her. . . . She has her own attitude to life. . . . I suppose everyone has. One can't exactly call her authoritarian, but she does like to have everything happen according to her wishes."

"After your father left, did you get on well with her?"

"More or less well . . . All the same I was glad to get married and . . ."

"And escape from her authority?"

"Something of that sort . . ."

She smiled. "It's not at all special, and a great many girls are in the same position. My mother loves going out, entertaining, meeting important people. . . . In Mulhouse everyone of any consequence in the town used to come to her parties."

"Even in your father's time?"

"During the last two years, yes . . ."

"Why the last two?"

He remembered Madame Maigret's lengthy telephone conversation with her sister and felt a bit sorry that he was learning more here than his wife would find out.

"Because Mother had inherited some money from her aunt. Before that, we lived quite humbly, in a small house. . . . We weren't even in one of the better-class districts, and my father's practice was chiefly working class. . . . None of us expected this inheritance. We moved . . . Mother bought a large house near the cathedral and she wasn't sorry that there was a coat of arms carved over the doorway."

"Did you know your father's family?"

"No . . . I'd only seen his brother a certain number of times before he was killed in the war, in Syria, I believe, at any rate not in France."

"His father? His mother?"

Children's voices could be heard again, but this time she took no notice.

"His mother died of cancer when my father was about fifteen. . . . His father had a carpenters' and joiners' business. . . . One fine day, while my father was still at university, he was found hanging in the workshop, and it turned out that he was on the verge of bankruptcy."

"But your father managed nonetheless to finish his studies?"

"By working in a pharmacy . . ."

"What was he like?"

"Very gentle . . . I know this hardly answers your question, but that's the chief impression he left on me. . . . Very gentle and rather sad . . ."

"Did he quarrel with your mother?"

"I never heard him raise his voice. . . . It's true that when he was not in his office he spent most of his time visiting patients. . . . I remember Mother scolding him for not taking care of his appearance, for always wearing the same crumpled suit and sometimes going without shaving for three days. . . . I used to tell him his beard was prickly when he kissed me."

"I suppose you know nothing about your father's relations with his colleagues?"

"All that I know comes through Mother. . . . Only, with her, it's difficult to distinguish what's true from what's more or less true. . . . She doesn't tell lies. . . . She arranges the truth so that it bears some resemblance to what she'd like it to be. Since she had married my father, he had to be somebody quite remarkable.

" 'Your father's the best doctor in the town,' she used to tell me, 'probably one of the best in France. Unfortunately . . .' "

She smiled once more.

"You can guess the rest. . . . He couldn't adapt. . . . He refused to behave like other people. . . . She let it be understood that if my grandfather had hanged himself it was not because of imminent bankruptcy but because of mental depression. . . . He had a daughter who spent some time in a mental home. . . ."

"What became of her?"

"I don't know. . . . I don't think my mother knows, either. In any case, she left Mulhouse."

"Does your mother still live there?"

"She's been living in Paris for a long time now. . . ."

"Can you give me her address?"

"It's 29b Quai d'Orléans. . . ."

Maigret gave a start, but she did not notice.

"It's in the Ile Saint-Louis. Since the island became one of the most fashionable parts of Paris . . ."

"Do you know where your father was attacked last night?"

"Of course not."

"Under the Pont Marie . . . three hundred yards from your mother's home . . ."

She knit her brows anxiously.

"It's on the other branch of the Seine, isn't it? Mother's windows look out on to the Quai des Tournelles. . . ."

"Has she a dog?"

"Why do you ask that?"

During the few months that Maigret had spent in Place des Vosges, while the house on the Boulevard Richard-Lenoir was undergoing alterations, he and his wife used often to take a walk in the evenings round the Ile Saint-Louis. That was when dog owners or their servants used to walk their animals along the embankment.

"Mother has only birds. . . . She detests dogs and cats. . . ."

And, changing the subject:

"Where has my father been taken to?"

"To the Hôtel Dieu, the nearest hospital . . ."

"I suppose you'd like me to . . ."

"Not just yet . . . I may perhaps ask you to come and identify him, so that we may be absolutely certain, but for the moment his head and face are covered with bandages. . . ."

"Is he in much pain?"

"He's in a coma and not conscious of anything. . . ."

"Why did they do such a thing?"

"That's what I'm trying to find out."

"Was there a fight?"

"No. In all probability he was attacked while he was sleeping."

"Underneath the bridge?"

Maigret now rose.

"I suppose you're going to see Mother?"

"I'm afraid I shall have to. . . ."

"May I ring her up and tell her the news?"

He hesitated. He would have preferred to watch Madame Keller's reactions. However, he did not insist.

"Thank you, Superintendent. Will it be in the papers?"

"There'll have been a brief report of the assault by now, but your father's name will certainly not appear in it, for I only learned it myself in the middle of the morning."

"Mother won't want it talked about. . . ."

"I'll do my best. . . ."

She went with him to the front door, while a small girl clung to her skirt.

"We're going out right away now, darling. . . . Go and ask Nanny to dress you."

Torrence was pacing up and down the pavement in front of the house, and the little black police car cut a poor figure among the long gleaming cars of the local residents.

"Quai des Orfèvres?"

"No . . . Ile Saint-Louis . . . Quai d'Orléans."

The house was an old one, with a huge carriage gate-way, but it was as well cared for as a piece of valuable furniture. The brasswork, the handrail of the stairs, the steps and walls were clean and polished, without a speck of dust; the concierge herself, in a black dress and white apron, looked like a maid from some upper-class house-hold.

"Have you an appointment?"

"No. Madame Keller is expecting me."

"One moment, please . . ."

The lodge was a little parlor that smelled of polish rather than of cooking. The concierge picked up the telephone.

"What is your name?"

"Superintendent Maigret . . ."

"Hullo . . . Berthe . . . Would you tell Madame that a certain Superintendent Maigret is asking to see her? . . . Yes, he's right here. . . . Can he go up? . . . Thanks . . . You can go up. . . Second floor on the right."

Maigret wondered, as he climbed the stairs, whether the Flemings' boat was still moored at the Quai des Célestins or whether, the statement having been duly signed, they were already traveling downstream toward Rouen. The door opened without his having to ring. The maid, young and pretty, examined the superintendent from head to foot, as if it were the first time in her life that she had seen a real live detective.

"This way . . . Let me take your hat."

The apartment was high-ceilinged and decorated in baroque style, with a great deal of gilt and richly carved furniture. From the entrance hall he could hear the chirping of budgerigars, and when the living-room door was opened he beheld a huge cage with almost a dozen pairs of birds in it.

He waited for about ten minutes, and finally by way of protest lit his pipe. However, he removed it from his mouth when Madame Keller made her entry. It came as a surprise to find her so tiny, so fragile-looking, and yet so young; she seemed barely ten years older than her daughter. She was dressed in black and white and had a fresh complexion and forget-me-not blue eyes.

"Jacqueline called me," she said immediately, waving Maigret toward an armchair with a high upright back, as uncomfortable as possible. She herself sat on a stool covered in antique tapestry, holding herself as she must have been taught to at her convent school.

"So you've found my husband . . ."

"We weren't looking for him. . . ." he retorted.

"I'm sure . . . There's no reason why you should have been looking for him. . . . Everyone's free to live as he chooses. . . . Is it true that his life is not in danger, or did you tell my daughter that to spare her feelings?"

"Doctor Magnin thinks he has an 80 per cent chance of recovering."

"Magnin? I know him quite well. . . . He's often been here."

"Did you know your husband was in Paris?"

"I knew it without really knowing it. . . . Since he left for Gabon nearly twenty years ago I have had two postcards from him, and that's all. . . . And that was right at the beginning of his stay in Africa."

She made no pretense of grief, but looked him squarely

in the face, as a woman familiar with every kind of situation would.

"Are you sure, at least, that it's really him?"

"Your daughter recognized him. . . ."

He showed her, too, the identity card with its photograph. She fetched her glasses from the top of a chest of drawers and examined the portrait attentively, her face betraying not the least trace of emotion.

"Jacqueline was quite right. . . . Of course, he's changed, but I'd swear, too, that it's François. . . ."

She looked up.

"Is it true that he lived a few steps away from here?"

"Under the Pont Marie . . ."

"And to think that I cross that bridge several times a week, for I have a friend who lives just the other side of the Seine. . . . Madame Lambois . . . You must know the name . . . her husband . . ."

Maigret did not wait to be told of the important position held by Madame Lambois's husband.

"You've not seen your husband again since the day he left Mulhouse?"

"Never."

"Did he never write to you or telephone you?"

"Apart from the two postcards, I never had any news of him. . . . At any rate, not directly . . ."

"And indirectly?"

"I did happen to meet, at a friend's house, a former governor of Gabon, Pérignon by name, who asked me whether I was related to a certain Dr. Keller. . . ."

"What did you reply?"

"I told him the truth. . . . He looked embarrassed. . . .

I had to worm it out of him. . . . At last he admitted that François had failed to find what he was seeking for out there. . . ."

"What was he seeking for?"

"He was an idealist, do you see? . . . He was not cut out for modern life. . . . After his disappointment at Mulhouse . . ."

Maigret showed some surprise.

"Did my daughter not tell you about it? . . . It's true that she was very young and saw so little of her father. . . . Instead of acquiring the practice he deserved . . . Will you take a cup of tea? . . . No? . . . Excuse me for having some in front of you, but it's my tea time. . . ."

She rang the bell.

"My tea, Berthe . . ."

"For one?"

"Yes . . . What can I offer you, Superintendent? . . . Some whisky? . . . Nothing? Just as you please . . . What was I saying? . . . Oh, yes. Didn't someone write a novel called *The Poor Man's Doctor?* Or am I thinking of *The Country Doctor?* Well, my husband was a kind of poor man's doctor, and if I hadn't inherited money from my aunt we should have become as poor as his patients. . . . Not that I'm blaming him for it. . . . It was in his nature. . . . His father . . . well, no matter . . . Every family has its problems."

The telephone rang.

"Excuse me . . . Hullo . . . Yes, speaking . . . Alice? . . . Yes, darling . . . I may be a little late. . . . Oh, no! . . . Very well, on the contrary . . . Have you seen Laure? . . . She'll be there? . . . I won't go on now, because I

61

have a visitor. . . . I'll tell you all about it. . . . I'll see you presently. . . ."

She came back to her place, smiling.

"That was the wife of the Minister of the Interior. . . . Do you know her?"

Maigret merely shook his head and instinctively put his pipe back into his pocket. The budgerigars irritated him. So did the interruptions. The next thing was the maid bringing in tea.

"He'd got it into his head to become a hospital doctor and for two years he worked hard for the competitive examination. . . . Everyone in Mulhouse would tell you it was flagrantly unfair. . . . François was certainly the best and cleverest doctor there. . . . And I think he would have felt in the right place. . . . As usual, they appointed the protégé of one of the departmental heads. . . . But that was no reason for giving everything up. . . ."

"And it was as a result of this disappointment . . ."

"I suppose so. . . . I saw so little of him . . . When he was at home, he would shut himself up in his consulting room. . . . He had always been rather unsociable, but from that time on he seemed to go off the track completely. . . . I don't want to say anything unkind about him. . . . It never even occurred to me to divorce him when he wrote to suggest this. . . ."

"Did he drink?"

"Did my daughter say so?"

"No."

"He started drinking, yes . . . not that I ever saw him the worse for drink . . . But he always had a bottle in his consulting room and he was frequently seen coming out of little *bistrots* not usually frequented by a man in his position. . . ."

"You had begun to tell me about Gabon . . ."

"I think he wanted to become a sort of Dr. Schweitzer, if you see what I mean. . . . To go and look after Negroes in the wilds, to set up a hospital there and see as little as possible of white men, of people of his own class . . ."

"And was he disappointed?"

"From what the governor confided to me reluctantly, he succeeded in antagonizing the administration and the leading companies. . . . Perhaps on account of the climate, he took to drinking more and more. . . . Don't imagine I'm telling you this out of jealousy. . . . I've never been jealous. . . . Out there he lived in a native hut with a black woman and apparently had children by her. . . ."

Maigret stared at the budgerigars in the sunlit cage.

"They gave him to understand that he was unsuited to the post. . . ."

"You mean he was turned out of Gabon?"

"More or less . . . I don't know exactly how these things are done, and the governor was rather vague about it. . . . The fact remains that he left. . . ."

"How long ago was it that one of your friends met him in the Boulevard Saint-Michel?"

"Did my daughter tell you about that? Not that I can be sure of it . . . The man, who was carrying a board on his back advertising a local restaurant, looked like François, and apparently he gave a start when my friend addressed him by his name. . . ."

"Did your friend not speak to him?"

"François stared at him as if he did not recognize him. . . . That's all I know."

"As I told your daughter just now, I cannot ask you to come and identify him yet, because his face is covered with bandages. . . . As soon as there is some improvement . . ."

"Don't you think it may be painful?"

"For whom?"

"I'm thinking of him. . . ."

"We have to make sure of his identity."

"I'm practically certain . . . if only because of the scar . . . It was one Sunday in August . . ."

"I know."

"In that case, I don't see what else I have to tell you. . . ."

He rose, longing to get outside and away from the chattering budgerigars.

"I suppose the papers . . ."

"The papers will say as little as possible; that I can promise you."

"It's not so much for my own sake as for my son-in-law's. For a businessman it's always unpleasant to . . . even though he knows all about it and has understood the situation very well . . . Can I really not offer you anything?"

"No, thanks."

And on the pavement he said to Torrence, "Where can we find a quiet little *bistrot?* I've such a thirst!"

A glass of very cold beer with a creamy head to it!

They found the *bistrot*, as quiet and dark as they could have wished, but, alas, the beer was lukewarm and flat.

FOUR

Y ou'll find the list on your desk," said Lucas, who as usual had done a meticulous job.

There were, in fact, several typewritten lists. First, that of the various objects (classified under the heading "Unclaimed Articles" by the specialist of the police records department) found under the Pont Marie and constituting the entire worldly goods of François Keller. The whole lot—old boxes, baby carriage, torn blankets, newspapers, frying pan, mess tin, Bossuet's *Oraisons Funèbres*, and the rest—were now upstairs in a corner of the laboratory.

The second list was that of the clothes which Lucas had brought back from the Hôtel Dieu, and a third, finally, inventoried the contents of the pockets.

Maigret preferred not to read it, and it was odd to see him, in the light of the setting sun, opening the brown paper bag in which the police sergeant had put the small articles. His expression was rather like that of a child opening a surprise packet and expecting to find heaven knows what treasure.

The first thing he drew out was a dilapidated stethoscope, which he laid on his blotter.

"That was in the right-hand pocket of his jacket," observed Lucas. "I inquired at the hospital. It doesn't work."

In that case, why had François Keller carried it about with him? In the hope of getting it mended? Wasn't it rather as a last remaining symbol of his profession?

Next came a pocket knife with three blades and a corkscrew; its horn handle was cracked. Like the rest, it must have come out of some garbage heap.

A brier pipe, the stem of which had been mended with wire.

"Left-hand pocket," recited Lucas. "It's still damp."

Maigret sniffed at it instinctively.

"No tobacco?" he queried.

"You'll find a few cigarette ends at the bottom of the bag. They got so soaked that they're nothing but a mush."

You could picture the man pausing on the pavement and bending down to pick up a cigarette butt, taking off the paper and poking the tobacco into his pipe. Secretly, Maigret was pleased to find that the Doc was a pipe smoker. Neither the wife nor the daughter had mentioned this detail.

Nails and screws. What for? The tramp must have picked them up on his rounds and thrust them into his pocket without giving a thought to their use, probably considering them as talismans.

The proof of which was that there were three objects of even less use to someone who lies under the bridges with newspaper wrapped around his chest to keep out the cold: three marbles, those glass marbles in which you see yellow, red, blue, and green threads, the sort a child will swap for five or six ordinary marbles for the pleasure of seeing it shimmer in the sun.

That was practically all, except for a few coins and, in a leather wallet, two fifty-franc notes stuck together by the water of the Seine.

Maigret kept one of the marbles in his hand and during the rest of the conversation rolled it about between his fingers.

"Have you taken the fingerprints?"

"The other patients watched me with great interest. I went up to check them in the files department."

"What did you find out?"

"Nothing. Keller has never been involved with us or with the law."

"Has he recovered consciousness?"

"No. When I was there, his eyes were half open, but he didn't appear to be seeing anything. His breathing is a bit wheezy. From time to time he gives a moan. . . ."

Before going home the superintendent signed letters. In spite of his preoccupied air there was a certain light-heartedness about his mood, to match that of the air over Paris. Was it by accident that on leaving his office he slipped a marble into his pocket?

It was a Tuesday—macaroni au gratin for supper. Apart from Thursday's *pot-au-feu*, the menu varied from week to week, but for years now, for no apparent reason, Tuesday's evening meal had consisted of macaroni and cheese with minced ham in it and occasionally a finely sliced truffle.

Madame Maigret, too, was in a lively mood, and from the sparkle in her eyes he gathered that she had some news for him. He did not tell her right away that he had seen Jacqueline Rousselet and Madame Keller.

"I'm hungry!"

She expected questions. He did not ask any until they were both seated at table in front of the open window. The air was bluish, with a few lingering trails of red low down in the sky.

"Did your sister call you back?"

"I think she's done a good job. She must have spent the whole afternoon calling up all her friends."

She had a piece of paper with notes on it beside her plate.

"Shall I tell you what she said?"

The noises of the city made a resonant background to their conversation, and they could hear the beginning of the television news talk from their neighbors' apartment.

"Don't you want to turn on the news?"

"I'd rather listen to you."

Two or three times while she was speaking he put his hand into his pocket to play with the marble.

"What are you smiling at?"

"At nothing . . . I'm listening."

"To begin with, I know where the money came from that Madame Keller inherited from her aunt. . . . It's a longish story. . . . Shall I tell it to you in detail?"

He nodded while munching the crisp macaroni.

"She was a nurse, and still unmarried at forty-five."

"Did she live in Mulhouse?"

"No, Strasbourg . . . She was Madame Keller's mother's sister. . . . D'you follow me?"

"Yes."

"She worked at the hospital . . . The head men there each have a certain number of rooms at their disposal for their private patients. . . . One day, shortly before World War II, she had to nurse a man about whom there's been a lot of talk in Alsace since, a certain Lemke, a dealer in scrap metal who had already made a good deal of money and had rather a bad reputation. . . . He was said to be involved in usury. . . ."

"And he married her?"

"How did you know?"

He felt sorry for having spoiled her story.

"I guessed it from your expression."

"Yes, he married her. Wait for the next bit. During the war he kept up his trade in nonferrous metals. . . . Inevitably he had to deal with the Germans, and he amassed a considerable fortune. . . . Am I being long-winded? Am I boring you?"

"Quite the contrary. What happened at the Liberation?"

"The French Forces of the Interior hunted for Lemke to squeeze the money out of him and then to shoot him. . . . He was never caught. Nobody knows where he and his wife were hiding. Anyhow, they managed to reach Spain and from there they sailed to Argentina. . . . A mill owner from Mulhouse met Lemke over there in the street. . . . A little more macaroni?"

"Yes, please . . . some of the crispy top."

"I don't know whether he was still doing business or whether the couple were traveling for pleasure. . . . One day they took a plane to Brazil, and the aircraft crashed into the mountains. The crew and all the passengers were killed. . . . And it was precisely because Lemke and his wife died in a disaster that the money went to Madame Keller, who never expected it. . . . In the normal way it should have gone to the husband's relatives. . . . D'you know why the Lemkes got nothing and the wife's niece inherited the whole estate?"

He shook his head; he was cheating, for in fact he had understood.

"Apparently when a man and wife are victims of the same accident, so that it can't be established which of the two died first, the law assumes that the wife outlived her husband, even if only by a few moments. . . . The doctors' theory is that we are tougher than men; so the aunt inherited the fortune first, and then it went to her niece. . . . Phew!"

She seemed pleased and rather proud of herself.

"So that, all things considered, it was partly because a nurse married a scrap-metal merchant in a Strasbourg hospital, and a plane crashed in the mountains of South America, that Dr. Keller became a down-and-out. . . . If his wife hadn't become rich overnight, if they'd gone on living in the Rue du Sauvage, if . . . You see what I mean? Don't you believe, yourself, that he'd have stayed in Mulhouse?"

"Maybe . . ."

"I've got some information about her, too, but I warn you it's only gossip, and my sister denies all responsibility for it."

"Go on, tell me . . ."

"She's a lively little person, always on the go, who

adores social occasions and who's a regular lion hunter.
. . . Once her husband had left her, she went in for it
to her heart's content, organizing big dinner parties
several times a week. . . . In this way she came to have
a great influence on the Chief Commissioner, whose name
is Badet and whose wife (she's since died) was an in-
valid. . . . Scandalmongers assert that she was his mis-
tress and that she's had other lovers, including a general
whose name I've forgotten. . . ."

"I've seen her. . . ."

If Madame Maigret was disappointed, she showed no
sign of it.

"What's she like?"

"Just as you've described her . . . A lively, restless
little lady, very well groomed, looking younger than
her age and addicted to budgerigars . . ."

"Why d'you bring in budgerigars?"

"Because her apartment is full of them."

"Does she live in Paris?"

"In the Ile Saint-Louis, three hundred yards from the
Pont Marie, under which her husband used to sleep . . .
By the way, he smoked a pipe. . . ."

Between macaroni and salad, he had taken the marble
out of his pocket and was rolling it about the table.

"What's that?"

"A marble. The Doc had three of them. . . ."

She was watching her husband attentively.

"You're fond of him, aren't you?"

"I think I'm beginning to understand him. . . ."

"You can understand how a man like that can become
a tramp?"

"Perhaps . . . He'd lived in Africa, the only white man in a station remote from towns and main roads . . . And there, too, he was disappointed. . . ."

"Why?"

It was hard to explain this to Madame Maigret, who had always lived in clean and orderly surroundings.

"What I'm trying to guess," he went on lightly, "is what he could have been guilty of. . . ."

She knit her brows.

"What do you mean? Surely it was he who was knocked out and thrown into the Seine?"

"He was the victim, true. . . ."

"Well, then? Why do you say . . ."

"Criminologists, particularly American criminologists, have a theory on the subject, and it's maybe not as extravagant as it sounds. . . ."

"What theory?"

"That in eight out of ten crimes the victim is to a large extent as responsible as the murderer. . . ."

"I don't understand. . . ."

He was staring at the marble as though it fascinated him.

"Take the case of a quarrel between a woman and a jealous man . . . The man accuses the woman, who taunts him . . ."

"That must sometimes happen. . . ."

"Suppose he's holding a knife in his hand and says to her, 'Take care . . . Next time, I'll kill you . . .' "

"That must sometimes happen, too."

But not in the world she knew!

"Suppose, now, that she jeers at him: 'You wouldn't dare! You're not capable of it.' "

"I see what you mean."

"Well, in many crimes of passion, there's something of that sort. . . . You were talking about Lemke, who made his fortune partly by usury, driving his clients to desperation, and partly by trading with the Germans. . . . Would you have been surprised to learn that he had been murdered?"

"The doctor . . ."

"He seemed to do no harm to anyone. He lived under the bridges, drank red wine straight out of the bottle and walked the streets with an advertisement board on his back. . . ."

"Well, then!"

"And yet somebody went down on to the riverbank at night and took advantage of his being asleep to deal him a blow on the head that might have been fatal, then dragged him along and threw him into the Seine, from which he was rescued only by a miracle. . . . That person had a motive. . . . In other words, the Doc had consciously or unconsciously given him a motive for putting him out of the way."

"Is he still in a coma?"

"Yes."

"Are you hoping that when he can speak you'll get something out of him?"

He shrugged his shoulders and began to fill his pipe. Soon afterward they put out the light and remained there, sitting by the open window.

It was a pleasant, peaceful evening, with long pauses between remarks, which did not prevent them from feeling very close to one another.

When Maigret reached his office next morning, the

weather was as radiant as the previous day, and the tiny green specks on the trees had already given way to real little delicate leaves.

The superintendent had barely sat down at his desk when Lapointe came in, in high spirits.

"I've got two customers for you, Chief. . . ."

"Where are they?"

"In the waiting room."

"Who are they?"

"The owner of the red Peugeot and the friend who was with him on Monday night. . . . I don't take much credit for it. . . . Contrary to what you might expect, there aren't many red 403's in Paris and only three whose license plates include two nines. . . . One of those three has been under repair for the past week, and the other is at the present moment in Cannes with its owner. . . ."

"Have you questioned the men?"

"I asked them only one or two questions. . . . I thought it best for you to see them yourself. Shall I bring them in?"

There was something mysterious about Lapointe's attitude, as if he had another surprise in store for Maigret..

"Go ahead . . ."

He waited, sitting at his desk, with the multicolored marble still in his pocket, like a talisman.

"Monsieur Jean Guillot . . ." announced the inspector, ushering in the first customer.

This was a man of about forty, of average height, dressed with a certain studied smartness.

"Monsieur Hardoin, industrial draftsman . . ."

The second man was taller and thinner and several

years younger, and Maigret was soon to discover that he stammered.

"Sit down, messieurs . . . I understand that one of you is the owner of a red Peugeot. . . ."

Jean Guillot raised his hand, not without a certain pride.

"It's my car," he said. "I bought it at the beginning of the winter. . . ."

"Where do you live, Monsieur Guillot?"

"Rue de Turenne, not far from the Boulevard du Temple."

"Your profession?"

"Insurance agent."

He was somewhat awestruck at finding himself in police headquarters, being interrogated by a chief superintendent, but he showed no signs of fear. He even stared about him with curiosity, as though planning to describe the scene in detail to his friends later.

"And you, Monsieur Hardoin?"

"I—I—I . . . live in the same h—h—house."

"The floor above ours," Guillot helped him out.

"Are you married?"

"A b—b—b—bachelor . . ."

"*I'm* married with two children, a boy and a girl," Guillot put in again without waiting for questions.

Lapointe, standing by the door, was smiling vaguely. The two men, each sitting on a chair with his hat on his knees, looked like two performers in an act.

"You are friends?"

They replied as simultaneously as Hardoin's stutter would allow:

"Very good friends . . ."

"Do you know François Keller?"

They looked at one another in surprise, as if hearing the name for the first time. It was the draftsman who asked:

"Who—who—who's that?"

"He practiced medicine in Mulhouse for a long time."

"I've never set foot in Mulhouse," declared Guillot. "Does he claim to know me?"

"What were you doing on Monday night?"

"As I told your inspector, I had no idea it was against the law . . ."

"Tell me in detail what you did . . ."

"When I got back from my round, about eight o'clock —I cover the western suburbs—my wife drew me into a corner so that the children shouldn't hear, and told me that Nestor . . ."

"Who is Nestor?"

"Our dog . . . a great Dane. . . . He was twelve years old and very gentle with the children, whom he'd known from birth, so to speak. . . . When they were babies, he used to lie at the foot of the cot, and I hardly dared go near. . . ."

"So, then, your wife told you . . ."

He went on, quite unruffled:

"I don't know if you've ever kept a great Dane. . . . In general, they don't live as long as other dogs—I can't think why—and when they grow old they suffer from nearly all the same weaknesses as men. . . . For the past few weeks Nestor had been almost paralyzed, and I'd suggested taking him to the vet to have an injection. . . ."

My wife hadn't wanted that. . . . When I got home on Monday, the dog was dying, and so the children shouldn't witness such a sight my wife had brought down our friend Lucien, who helped her to carry the dog up to his apartment. . . ."

Maigret glanced at Lapointe, who gave him a discreet wink.

"I went up to Hardoin's apartment immediately to see what was happening to the dog. Poor Nestor was about done for. I called the vet and was told he was at the theater and wouldn't be back before midnight. . . . For over two hours we stayed there watching the dog die. . . . I'd sat down on the ground, and he'd laid his head on my knees. . . . His body was shaking convulsively. . . ."

Hardoin was nodding in confirmation and trying to put in a word.

"He—he—"

"He died at half past ten," the insurance agent interrupted him. "I went down to tell my wife. I stayed to look after the apartment, where the children were asleep, while she went up to see Nestor for the last time. . . . I had a bite to eat, for I'd had no dinner. . . . I must confess I then drank a couple of glasses of brandy to steady me, and when my wife came back I took the bottle upstairs to give some to Hardoin, who was as upset as I was."

In fact, it had been a little drama in the shadow of another drama.

"And that was when we wondered what we were going to do with the body. . . . I've heard that there's a cemetery for dogs, but I suppose it costs a lot, and, besides, I can't afford to lose a day's work seeing to that. .... As for my wife, she hasn't the time . . ."

"In short . . ." said Maigret.

"In short . . ."

And Guillot paused, having lost the thread of his ideas.

"We . . . we . . . we . . ."

"We didn't want to dump him on a piece of waste ground. . . . Have you any idea of the size of a great Dane? Lying there in Hardoin's dining room, he looked even huger and more impressive. In short . . ."

He was relieved to have got back to that point.

"In short, we decided to put him into the Seine. I went back to our place to fetch a potato sack. . . . It wasn't big enough, and we couldn't get his paws in. . . . It was quite a job carrying him downstairs and putting him into the trunk of the car."

"What time was it?"

"Ten past eleven."

"How do you know it was ten past eleven?"

"Because the concierge hadn't gone to bed. She saw us go past and asked us what had happened. I explained to her. Her door was open, and I instinctively looked at the clock, which said ten past eleven."

"You told her you were going to throw the dog into the Seine? You drove directly to the Pont des Célestins?"

"It was the nearest . . ."

"It took you only a few minutes to get there. . . . I suppose you didn't stop on the way?"

"Not on the way there . . . We took the quickest route. . . . It must have taken us five minutes. . . . I wasn't keen on driving down the ramp. . . . As I saw nobody there, I took a chance."

"So it wasn't yet half past eleven?"

"Surely not . . . you'll see . . . We both took hold of the sack and we tipped it into the river. . . ."

"And you still saw nobody?"

"Nobody . . ."

"Was there a barge nearby?"

"That's true. . . . We even noticed a light inside."

"But you didn't see the bargeman?"

"No."

"You didn't go as far as the Pont Marie?"

"We had no reason to go any farther. . . . We threw Nestor into the water as close to the car as we could . . ."

Hardoin kept on nodding assent, sometimes opening his mouth to put in a word and then closing it again, discouraged.

"What happened next?"

"We went away. . . . Once we were up there . . ."

"On the Quai des Célestins, you mean?"

"Yes . . . I didn't feel too good and I remembered there was no more brandy in the bottle. . . . It had all been quite an ordeal. . . . Nestor was almost one of the family. In Rue de Turenne, I suggested to Lucien that we have a drink, and we stopped at a café on the corner of Rue des Francs-Bourgeois, close to the Place des Vosges. . . ."

"You had some more brandy?"

"Yes . . . There was a clock there, too, and I looked at it. . . . The proprietor pointed out that it was five minutes fast . . . it was twenty to twelve. . . ."

He repeated, with a crestfallen air:

"I swear to you I didn't know it wasn't allowed. . . . Put yourself in my place. . . . It was chiefly for the children's sake, because I wanted to spare them the sight. They still don't know that the dog is dead. We've told them he's gone away, that he might turn up again perhaps. . . ."

Unconsciously, Maigret had pulled the marble out of his pocket and was fingering it.

"I suppose you've told me the truth?"

"Why should I tell you a lie? If there's a fine to be paid, I'm ready to . . ."

"What time did you get home?"

The two men glanced at one another in some confusion. Once again Hardoin opened his mouth, and once again it was Guillot who answered.

"Late . . . about one in the morning . . ."

"Did the café in Rue de Turenne stay open until one in the morning?"

It was a district that Maigret knew well, where everything shuts at midnight or even a good deal earlier.

"No, we went for a last drink in the Place de la Republique."

"Were you drunk?"

"You know how it is. . . . You drink because you're upset. . . . One glass, then another . . ."

"You didn't go back along the Seine?"

Guillot looked surprised and glanced at his companion as though asking him to confirm his evidence.

"Oh, no! Why should we?"

Maigret turned to Lapointe.

"Take them next door and file their statements. Thank you, gentlemen . . . I need not tell you that we shall check up on everything you've told us."

"I swear to you I've told the truth . . ."

"So—so—so have I!"

There was something farcical about it. Maigret was left alone in his room, standing in front of the open window with the glass marble in his hand. In a brown study, he watched the Seine flowing beneath the trees, the boats passing, and the women's dresses making light patches on the Pont Saint-Michel.

At last he sat down again and rang up the Hôtel Dieu.

"I'd like to speak to the sister in charge of the surgical ward."

Now that she had seen him with the big chief himself and had been given her instructions, she was all honey.

"I was just about to ring you, Superintendent. . . . Doctor Magnin has just examined him. . . . He finds him much better than last night and hopes that complications can be avoided. . . . It's almost a miracle. . . ."

Has he recovered consciousness?"

"Not quite, but he's beginning to look about him and to show some interest. It's hard to say if he's aware of his condition and of his surroundings."

"Has he still got his bandages on?"

"Not on the face . . ."

"Do you think he'll recover consciousness today?"

"It may happen at any moment. . . . Would you like me to get in touch with you as soon as he speaks?"

"No . . . I'm coming over."

"Now?"

Now, yes. He was eager to make the acquaintance of the man whom he had seen hitherto only with his head bandaged. He went through the inspectors' room, where

Lapointe was busy typing out the statements of the insurance agent and his stuttering friend.

"I'm off to the Hôtel Dieu. . . . I don't know when I'll be back. . . ."

It was almost next door. He walked there as though for a neighborly call, taking his time, his pipe between his teeth and his hands behind his back, with vague thoughts floating through his mind.

When he reached the Hôtel Dieu, he saw Big Léa, still wearing her pink blouse, walking away from the reception desk with a resentful look on her face. She hurried to meet him.

"You know, Superintendent, they not only keep me from seeing him but they refuse to give me news of him. . . . They nearly fetched a policeman to throw me out. . . . Have you got any news of him yourself?"

"I've just heard that he's a lot better."

"Do they think he's going to pull through?"

"It's quite likely."

"Is he in much pain?"

"I don't think he's conscious of it. . . . I imagine they've given him an injection."

"Yesterday some plain-clothes men came to collect his things. Were they your people?"

He answered in the affirmative, and added with a smile:

"You needn't worry. . . . He'll get everything back."

"You've still got no idea who could have done such a thing?"

"And have you?"

"I've lived on the embankment fifteen years now, and this is the first time anyone's attacked a vagrant. For one thing, we're harmless people; you must know that better than anyone. . . ."

She was pleased with the word, and she repeated it:

"Harmless . . . There aren't even any fights, ever. . . . Each of us respects the other's liberty. If we didn't respect each other's liberty, why should we sleep underneath the bridges?"

He scrutinized her more closely and noticed that her eyes were somewhat redder, her color higher than on the previous day.

"Have you been drinking?"

"To get rid of the blues . . ."

"What have your friends been saying?"

"They haven't said anything. When you've seen all there is to see, you don't bother with gossip."

As Maigret was about to go in, she asked him:

"Can I wait till you come out to have some news of him?"

"I may be a long time. . . ."

"It doesn't matter. . . . I may as well be here as anywhere else."

She had recovered her good humor, her childish smile.

"You wouldn't have a cigarette on you?"

He indicated his pipe.

"Well, then, a pinch of tobacco . . . I chew it if I can't smoke."

He went up in the elevator at the same time as a patient on a stretcher and two nurses. On the third floor he met the ward sister coming out of one of the wards.

"You know the way. . . . I'll be with you in a moment. . . . They've rung for me from Emergencies. . . ."

The patients lying in their beds turned to look at him,

as on the previous day. Already, they seemed to recognize him. He made his way to Dr. Keller's bed, hat in hand, and at last discovered a face on which only a few strips of plaster remained.

The man, who had been shaved the day before, bore little resemblance to his photograph. His face was sunken, his skin colorless, his lips thin and pale. What struck Maigret above all was to find a man's gaze suddenly confronting him.

For there was no doubt about it: the Doc was looking at him, and the gaze was not that of an unconscious man.

It embarrassed him to stand there, silent. On the other hand, he did not know what to say. There was a chair beside the bed, and he sat down on it, murmuring uneasily, "Are you feeling better?"

He was convinced that the words did not vanish into mist, that they had been noted and understood. But there was not a flicker in the eyes that remained fixed on him; they expressed nothing but complete indifference.

"Do you hear me, Dr. Keller?"

It was the start of a long, frustrating struggle.

Maigret seldom talked to his wife about an inquiry when it was under way. In fact he avoided discussing it with his closest collaborators, to whom he would merely give instructions. This was all part of his way of working, his attempts to understand, to immerse himself gradually in the way of life of people unknown to him the previous day.

"What do you think about it, Maigret?" an examining magistrate would often ask him during a visit from the public prosecutor's department or the reconstitution of a crime.

His invariable reply was often quoted in the law courts:

"I never think, *monsieur le juge.*"

And somebody had added one day: "He's soaking it in. . . ." This was true, in a way; words were too precise for him, so that he preferred to keep silence.

This time it was different, at any rate with Madame Maigret, perhaps because, thanks to her sister, who lived in Mulhouse, she had lent him a helping hand. As they sat down to lunch, he announced:

"This morning I made Keller's acquaintance. . . ."

She was surprised, not only because he had broached the subject first but on account of the cheerfulness of his tone. That was not quite the right word, nor was it exactly sprightliness. Nonetheless, there was a certain light-hearted good humor in his voice and in his eyes.

For once, the papers were not harassing him, while the deputy public prosecutor and the examining magistrate had left him in peace. A tramp had been attacked under the Pont Marie and thrown into the flooded Seine, but he had survived as though by a miracle, and Dr. Magnin was astonished at his powers of recovery.

In short, it was a crime without a victim, one might almost have said without a murder, and nobody bothered much about the Doc except perhaps for Big Léa and two or three down-and-outs.

Maigret, however, devoted as much of his time to this affair as to some drama that aroused passionate interest throughout France. He seemed to have made it his personal concern, and from the way he had just announced his interview with Keller, he might have been speaking of somebody that he and his wife had been wanting to meet for a long time.

"Has he recovered consciousness?" asked Madame Maigret, trying not to display an excessive interest.

"Yes and no . . . He did not utter a word. He merely looked at me, but I'm convinced that he did not miss a word of what I said . . . The sister in charge doesn't share my opinion. . . . She maintains that he is still stupefied by the drugs he's been given and that he's like a punch-drunk boxer. . . ."

As he ate, he looked out of the window and listened to the birds.

"Do you get the impression that he knows who attacked him?"

Maigret sighed and finally gave a faint self-mocking smile that was uncharacteristic.

"I don't know. . . . I'd find it hard to explain my impression."

He had seldom in all his life felt as baffled as that morning in the Hôtel Dieu, or as passionately interested in any problem.

The conditions of the interview, for one thing, had hardly been favorable. It had taken place in a ward where a dozen patients were lying and three or four more sitting or standing by the window. Some of them were seriously ill and in pain, and there was a ceaseless ringing of bells and a coming and going of nurses, bending over one bed or another.

Everyone was staring more or less intently at the superintendent as he sat beside Keller, and all ears were on the alert.

Furthermore, the ward sister had appeared at the door from time to time, watching them uneasily and with obvious annoyance.

"You mustn't stay too long," she had advised him. "Don't tire him."

Maigret, bending over the sickbed, spoke gently in a low voice, so that a kind of murmur could be heard.

"Do you hear me, Monsieur Keller? Do you remember what happened to you on Monday night while you were lying under the Pont Marie?"

Not a feature of the injured man's face stirred, but the superintendent was concerned only with watching his eyes, which expressed neither distress nor anxiety. They were eyes of a washed-out gray color, which had seen a great deal and seemed almost worn out.

"Were you asleep when you were attacked?"

The Doc made no attempt to avert his gaze from Maigret, and a curious thing happened: it seemed as though Keller was scrutinizing his interlocutor, instead of the other way around.

This impression was so embarrassing that the superintendent felt impelled to introduce himself.

"My name's Maigret. . . . I'm in charge of the criminal squad of the Police Judiciaire. I'm trying to find out what happened to you. . . . I've seen your wife and your daughter, and the bargemen who pulled you out of the Seine."

The Doc gave no start at the mention of his wife and daughter, but Maigret could have sworn that a flicker of irony showed in his eyes.

"Are you unable to speak?"

The man made no effort to reply by even the slightest movement of the head or twitch of the eyelids.

"Are you conscious of being spoken to?"

Yes, yes! Maigret was convinced that he was right. Not only was Keller aware of his words, but he did not miss the least shade of their meaning.

"Does it bother you being questioned in the ward, with other patients listening to us?"

Then, almost coaxingly, he endeavored to explain:

"I should have liked you to be in a private room. . . . Unfortunately, that raises complicated administrative questions. Our budget doesn't allow us to pay for one."

Paradoxically, things would have been simpler if,

instead of being the victim, the doctor had been the aggressor or merely a suspect. There were no rules for dealing with victims.

"I am going to have to bring your wife here, for it's necessary that she should make a formal identification. . . . Shall you mind seeing her again?"

The lips moved slightly, without emitting a single sound, and there was neither a smile nor a grimace.

"Do you feel well enough for me to ask her to come in this morning?"

The man gave no sign of protest, and Maigret took advantage of this to allow himself a pause. He felt hot, almost stifled in the atmosphere of sickness and medicaments that pervaded the room.

He went to ask the ward sister if he could use the telephone.

"Are you going to keep on tormenting him?"

"His wife has got to identify him. It'll only take a few minutes."

He told the whole story, after a fashion, to Madame Maigret as they had their lunch in front of the window.

"She was at home," he went on. "She promised to come at once. I left instructions down below that she was to be allowed in. I walked about in the passage, where Dr. Magnin eventually joined me."

They had chatted together, standing in front of a window that overlooked the courtyard.

"Do you believe, as I do, that he's recovered his lucidity?" Maigret had asked.

"It's possible. . . . When I examined him just now, he gave me the impression of knowing what was happening round about him. But from a medical point of view I can't as yet give you a categorical answer. . . . People imagine that we are infallible and can answer every question. . . . But most of the time we're feeling our way. I asked a neurologist to have a look at him this afternoon."

"I suppose it would be difficult to put him in a private ward?"

"Not only difficult but impossible. Everything's full up. In some departments they've had to put beds in the corridors. . . . Or else he'd have to be taken to a private nursing home. . . ."

"Suppose his wife suggested it?"

"Do you think he'd like that himself?"

It was unlikely. If Keller had chosen to go off and live under the bridges, it was not in order to find himself, as the result of an assault, living at his wife's expense.

She, meanwhile, emerged from the elevator, looked round in bewilderment, and Maigret went to receive her.

"How is he?"

She displayed little anxiety or emotion. She seemed, above all, to be out of her element here and longing to get back as soon as possible to her apartment and her budgerigars on the Ile Saint-Louis.

"He's quite calm. . . ."

"Has he recovered consciousness?"

"I think so, but I cannot prove it. . . ."

"Am I to speak to him?"

He ushered her in ahead of him, and all the patients watched her walking across the polished floor of the ward. She, for her part, looked around for her husband, and of her own accord made her way toward the fifth bed, halting two or three yards from it as if she did not know what expression to assume.

Keller had seen her and was now watching her with unchanged indifference.

She was extremely elegant in her beige shantung suit, with a hat to match, and her perfume mingled with the hospital smells.

"Do you recognize him?"

"Yes, it's him. . . . He's changed, but it's him."

There was a fresh silence, which was trying for everyone. At last she made up her mind to go forward, with a certain bravery. Her gloved fingers nervously fiddling with the clasp of her bag, she said:

"It's me, François. . . . I didn't expect to meet you again some day in such wretched circumstances. . . . They tell me you're going to recover very quickly. I'd like to help you. . . ."

What was he thinking, as he fixed that gaze on her? For seventeen or eighteen years he had been living in another world. It was as if he was surfacing to find himself confronted with a past from which he had fled.

His face betrayed no sign of bitterness. He merely gazed at the woman who had been his wife for so long, then turned his head a little to make sure that Maigret was still there.

And now the latter was explaining to Madame Maigret:

"I'd take my oath that he was asking me to bring this confrontation to an end. . . ."

"You're talking about him as if you'd always known him. . . ."

Was this not true, in a way? Maigret had never met

Keller before, but during his career, how many confessions had he not listened to from men like Keller, in the privacy of his office? Perhaps not such extreme cases; but the human problem was the same, nonetheless.

"She did not insist on staying," he went on. "Before leaving him, she nearly opened her bag to take out some money. Fortunately, she didn't do so. . . . In the corridor she asked me:

" 'Do you think there's anything he needs?'

"And, as I said no, she persisted:

" 'I could perhaps hand over a certain sum for his benefit to the head of the hospital? . . . He'd be better in a private ward. . . .'

" 'There's not one available. . . .'

"She did not pursue the matter. 'What ought I to do?'

" 'Nothing for the moment . . . I shall send an inspector to get your signature to a statement acknowledging that this is in fact your husband. . . .'

" 'What's the point, since it *is* François?'

"She went away at last. . . ."

They had finished eating and were sitting in front of their cups of coffee. Maigret had lighted his pipe.

"Did you go back into the ward?"

"Yes . . . in spite of glares from the ward sister . . ."

He felt a kind of personal hostility toward her.

"Did he still not speak?"

"No . . . I went on talking to him in a low voice while a houseman was attending the patient in the next bed. . . ."

"What did you say to him?"

To Madame Maigret this conversation over the coffee cups was almost a miracle. Usually, she scarcely knew what cases her husband was dealing with. He would call her to say he'd not be back for lunch or for dinner, sometimes that he was going to spend half the night in his office or elsewhere, and usually it was through the newspapers that she gathered any further information.

"I can't remember what I said to him. . . ." he replied, somewhat uneasily. "I wanted to gain his confidence. I talked to him about Léa, who was waiting for me outside, about his possessions, which had been put away safely and which he would get back when he was discharged from hospital. . . . He seemed pleased at that.

"I also told him that he need not see his wife again if he didn't want to, that she had offered to pay for a private room for him but there was none available. . . .

"I must have looked, from a distance, as though I were reciting my prayers. . . .

" 'I assume you'd rather stay here than go into a nursing home?' "

"And did he still give no answer?"

Maigret looked embarrassed.

"I know it's silly, but I'm sure that he agreed with me, that we understood one another. . . . I tried to return to the subject of the assault. . . .

" 'Were you asleep?'

"We seemed to be playing cat and mouse. . . . I'm convinced that he has made up his mind once and for all to say nothing. And a man who has been capable of roughing it for so long is capable of holding his tongue. . . ."

"Why should he hold his tongue?"

"I don't know."

"To avoid accusing somebody?"

"Possibly."

"Whom?"

Maigret stood up, shrugging his broad shoulders.

"If I knew that, I should be the Lord Almighty. . . . I feel like giving you Dr. Magnin's answer: I don't work miracles either. . . ."

"So, all in all, you've learned nothing new?"

"No."

That was not strictly true. He was convinced that he had learned a great deal about the Doc. Even though he had not yet begun to know him really, certain secret and somewhat mysterious contacts seemed to have been made between them.

"At one point . . ."

He seemed reluctant to continue, as though he was afraid of being accused of childishness. Well, it couldn't be helped; he needed to talk.

"At one point, I took the marble out of my pocket. . . . Actually I didn't do so consciously. I felt it in my hand, and it occurred to me to slip it into his. . . . I probably must have appeared rather ridiculous. . . . But he didn't need to look at it. He recognized it by the feel. . . . I'm sure, whatever the sister may say, that his face lit up and there was a sparkle of joy and mischief in his eyes. . . ."

"And yet he never spoke?"

"That's another matter. . . . He's not going to help me. He's made up his mind not to help me, not to tell me anything, and I shall have to find out the truth by myself."

Was it the challenge that excited him? His wife had seldom seen him show such passionate and lively interest in a case.

"Downstairs, Léa was waiting for me on the pavement, chewing my tobacco, and I gave her what was left in my pouch. . . ."

"D'you suppose she knows anything?"

"If she did she would tell me. . . . There's a greater solidarity between these people than between those who live in the normal way, in houses. . . . I'm convinced that at this very moment they're discussing it among themselves, conducting their own investigation alongside mine. . . .

"I learned just one fact from her that might be of interest: Keller hasn't always slept under the Pont Marie and has belonged to that district, so to speak, only for the past two years. . . ."

"Where did he live before that?"

"On another part of the riverbank, higher up, on the Quai de la Rapée, under the Pont de Bercy . . ."

"Do they often change their quarters?"

"No. It's as much of a business as moving house for us. . . . Each of them chooses his own corner and sticks to it, more or less. . . ."

Finally, as though to reward himself or to maintain his good humor, he poured himself a small glass of sloe brandy. After which he picked up his hat and kissed Madame Maigret.

"See you this evening."

"D'you expect to be back for dinner?"

He did not know any more than she did. To tell the

truth, he had not the slightest idea what he was going to do.

Since that morning, Torrence had been checking the statements of the insurance agent and his stuttering friend. He must already have questioned Madame Goulet, the concierge in Rue de Turenne, and the wine merchant at the corner of Rue des Francs-Bourgeois.

They would soon know whether the story of the dog Nestor was true or a complete invention. And even if it was true, that would not prove that the two men had not attacked the Doc.

For what reason? At this stage of the inquiry Maigret could see none.

What reason might Madame Keller have had, for instance, for having her husband thrown into the Seine? And by whom?

One day, when a penniless and insignificant fellow had been killed in equally mysterious circumstances, Maigret had said to the examining magistrate:

"The have-nots just don't get murdered."

Down-and-outs don't get murdered, either. But somebody had in fact tried to get rid of François Keller.

Maigret stood on the platform of the bus, absent-mindedly listening to the whispered conversation of two lovers beside him, when a hypothesis occurred to him. It was the expression "have-nots" that had suggested it.

As soon as he was back in his office he called Madame Keller. She was not at home. The maid informed him that she was lunching in town with a friend, but didn't know in which restaurant.

Then he called Jacqueline Rousselet.

"I gather you've seen Mother. . . . She telephoned me last night, after your visit. She's just called me again, less than an hour ago. . . . So it really is my father."

"There appears to be no doubt about his identity."

"And you've still no idea why he was attacked. Could there have been a fight?"

"Was your father given to fighting?"

"He was the gentlest creature on earth, at least at the time when he was living with us, and I think he'd have let himself be struck without hitting back. . . ."

"Are you acquainted with your mother's business affairs?"

"What business affairs?"

"When she married, she was not rich, and she had no idea that she would become rich one day. . . . Nor had your father . . . I wonder, under the circumstances, whether they thought of drawing up a marriage settlement. . . . If not, they must have been married under the system of joint property holding, in which case your father could claim his half of the fortune."

"That's not the case . . ." she replied unhesitatingly.

"You're quite sure of that?"

"Mother will confirm it. . . . The lawyers raised the question at the time of my own marriage. . . . My father and mother retained control of their separate properties."

"Would it be indiscreet to ask your lawyer's name?"

"Maître Prijean, Rue de Bassano . . ."

"Many thanks . . ."

"Do you want me to go to the hospital?"

"Do you want to yourself?"

"I'm not sure that he would like a visit from me. . . . He said nothing to my mother. . . . Apparently he pretended not to recognize her."

"Perhaps, indeed, it would be better not to go. . . ."

He needed to feel that he was doing something, and he promptly called Maître Prijean. There was a lengthy argument, and he even had to produce the threat of a rogatory warrant signed by the examining magistrate, for the lawyer objected on grounds of professional secrecy.

"I am just asking you to tell me whether Monsieur and Madame Keller, of Mulhouse, were married under the system of separate property holding, and if you handled the settlement. . . ."

In the end there was a curt "yes," and the lawyer hung up.

In other words, François Keller actually was a have-not, who had no claims on the fortune amassed by the scrap-metal merchant, which had eventually come down to his wife.

The switchboard operator was somewhat surprised when the superintendent demanded:

"Put me through to the Suresnes lock. . . ."

"The lock?"

"Yes, the lock. They must have a phone there."

"O.K., Chief . . ."

Eventually, he got through to the head lock keeper and introduced himself.

"I suppose you keep a record of the boats that pass from one reach to another? I want to know where I can find a motor barge that must have gone through your lock late yesterday afternoon. . . . A Flemish name, *De Zwarte Zwaan* . . ."

"Yes, I know it. . . . Two brothers, a little fair-haired woman, and a baby . . . They went through on the last opening, and spent the night just below the gates."

"Have you any idea where they are now?"

"Wait a minute . . . They've got a good diesel and the stream is still pretty fast. . . ."

Maigret could hear him calculating, muttering the names of towns and villages to himself.

"If I'm not mistaken, they must have covered about sixty miles, which would bring them somewhere around Juziers. . . . In any case, they're likely to have gone beyond Poissy. . . . It depends how long they had to wait at the locks at Bougival and Carrière. . . ."

A few minutes later the superintendent was in the inspectors' room.

"Does anybody here know the Seine well?"

A voice asked: "Upstream or downstream?"

"Downstream . . . somewhere near Poissy . . . probably a bit beyond . . ."

"I do! I've got a small boat and I go down to Le Havre every year in the summer holidays. . . . I know the neighborhood of Poissy particularly well because that's where I dock my boat. . . ."

The speaker was Neveu, a detective of undistinguished petty bourgeois appearance whom Maigret had not suspected of such sporting proclivities.

"Take one of the cars in the yard. . . . You can drive me . . ."

The superintendent kept Neveu waiting, for Torrence

had just come back to report on the result of his inquiry.

"It's quite true that the dog died on Monday night," he declared. "Madame Guillot is still in tears when she talks about it. . . . The two men put the body into the trunk of the car and went to throw it into the Seine. . . . The people in the café in Rue de Turenne remember them. . . . . They came in a little before closing time."

"What time was that?"

"Shortly after half past eleven . . . Some card players were just finishing a game of *belote*, and the proprietor was waiting to pull down his shutters. . . . Madame Guillot also admitted shamefacedly that her husband had come home late, she didn't know how late for she'd fallen asleep, and that he was half drunk. . . . She felt obliged to assure me that this was most unusual, that it was because he'd been so upset. . . ."

Eventually Maigret took his seat beside Neveu in the car, which threaded its way toward the Porte d'Asnières.

"We can't follow the Seine all the way," the detective explained. "You're sure the barge has gone beyond Poissy?"

"So the head lock keeper says . . ."

They began to see open cars along the road, and sometimes the driver had a girl's arm round his waist. People were planting flowers in their gardens. At one point they saw a woman in a light blue dress feeding her hens.

Maigret sat drowsing with his eyes half closed, apparently uninterested in the landscape, and every time the Seine came into view Neveu would tell him where they had got to.

Thus they saw a number of boats peacefully traveling up or down the river. On one, a woman was washing her linen on deck; on a second, another woman held the tiller, with a child of three or four years sitting at her feet.

The car stopped at Meulan, where several barges were moored.

"What name did you say, Chief?"

"*De Zwarte Zwaan* . . . It means "The Black Swan.""

The inspector got out of the car, walked across the quayside and began a conversation with some bargemen; Maigret, from a distance, watched them gesticulating.

"They came past half an hour ago," Neveu announced, resuming his seat at the wheel. "As they're doing a good six miles an hour or more, they can't be far from Juziers now."

It was a little way beyond that village, by the island of Montalet, that they caught sight of the Belgian barge traveling downstream. They drove two or three hundred yards past it, and Maigret took up his position on the bank. Here, unconcerned lest he appear ridiculous, he started making great gestures.

Hubert, the younger of the two brothers, was at the wheel, a cigarette between his lips. He recognized the superintendent, went to lean over the hatchway and slowed down the engine. A moment later Jef van Houtte, tall and thin, appeared on deck, head first, then shoulders, finally his whole long gangling body.

"I've got to talk to you. . . ." the superintendent shouted, using his hands as a megaphone.

Jef made signs to show that he could hear nothing on account of the engine, and Maigret tried to explain that he must stop.

They were in the open countryside. About one mile away they could see red and gray roofs, white walls, a gas pump, and a gilt inn sign.

Hubert van Houtte reversed the engine. The young woman had now put her head through the hatchway and was evidently asking her husband what was happening.

A somewhat confused maneuver followed. From a distance it looked as if the two men were not in agreement. Jef, the elder, was pointing to the village, as though ordering his brother to make for it, while Hubert, at the tiller, was already proceeding toward the bank.

Since there was no alternative, Jef finally flung out a mooring rope, and Inspector Neveu, as an experienced sailor, caught hold of it with a certain pride. There were some bollards on the bank, and a few moments later the barge had come to a halt in the stream.

"What d'you want now?" shouted Jef, who looked furious.

The barge lay several yards from the bank, and he made no attempt to put down the landing plank.

"What's the idea, stopping the boat like that? It's the right way to have an accident, I can tell you that. . . ."

"I need to talk to you," Maigret retorted.

"You talked to me as much as you wanted to in Paris. . . . I've got nothing further to tell you."

"In that case, I shall be obliged to summon you to my office."

"What's that? Me go back to Paris without unloading my slates?"

Hubert, more accommodating, was motioning his brother to calm down. Eventually he flung the landing plank over to the bank and crossed it like an acrobat to make it sure.

"Don't mind him, monsieur. It's quite true what he says. You can't stop a boat just anywhere. . . ."

Maigret went on deck, feeling somewhat uneasy, since he did not know exactly what questions he was going to ask. Moreover, he was in the department of Seine-et-Oise, and according to regulations it was up to the Versailles police to get a rogatory warrant and question the Flemings.

"Say, are you going to keep us a long time?"

"I don't know."

"Because we're not going to spend the night here, you know. We've just time to get to Mantes before sunset.

"In that case, carry on with your journey. . . ."

"D'you want to come with us?"

"Why not?"

"Well, this is something new!"

"Do you hear, Neveu? Go on to Mantes with the car. . . ."

"What d'you think of this, Hubert?"

"There's nothing to be done, Jef. . . . With the police, it's no use getting angry. . . ."

The young woman's blonde head could still be seen on a level with the deck, and the babble of a child sounded down below. As on the previous day, a good smell of cooking rose from the living quarters.

The plank that served as a footbridge was withdrawn. Neveu, before getting back into the car, unfastened the mooring rope, which sent up a glittering shower as it splashed into the water.

"If you've got more questions to ask, I'm ready. . . ."

Once again, the chugging of the diesel could be heard, and the lapping of water against the hull.

Maigret, standing at the stern of the barge, was slowly filling his pipe and wondering what he was going to say.

SIX

You did tell me yesterday, didn't you, that the car was a red one?"

"Yes, monsieur" (he pronounced the word *mossieu*, as circus clowns do). "It was as red as the red on that flag. . . ."

He pointed to the Belgian flag, red, yellow, and black, waving above the stern of the boat.

Hubert was at the tiller, and the blonde young woman had gone back to her child down below. As for Jef, his face betrayed two conflicting feelings, between which he seemed torn. On the one hand, Flemish hospitality required him to give a decent welcome to the super-intendent, as to any other visitor, and even to offer him a small glass of gin; on the other hand, he was still annoyed at having been stopped in mid-journey and he considered this further interrogation as an insult to his dignity.

He cast a crafty look at the intruder, whose business suit and black hat looked out of place on board the boat.

As for Maigret, he felt somewhat ill at ease and still uncertain how to tackle his difficult interlocutor. He had a long acquaintance with men of this sort, simple and rather stupid, who assume that one wants to take advantage of their naïveté, and because they are mistrustful, quickly become aggressive, or else withdraw into stubborn mutism.

This was not the first time the superintendent had conducted an inquiry on board a barge, although he had not done so for a long time. He remembered, in particular, what used to be called a "stable boat," drawn along canals by a horse that spent the night on board with its master.

Those boats were built of wood and had a pleasant smell, due to the resin with which they were periodically coated. Inside they were as neat as any suburban bungalow.

Here, through the open door, he observed a more bourgeois interior, with heavy oak furniture, rugs, vases on embroidered mats and a profusion of gleaming brass.

"Where were you when you heard a noise on the quayside? You were busy working on the engine, I believe?"

Jef's pale eyes were fixed on Maigret and he seemed to be still undecided about what attitude to adopt, fighting down his anger.

"See here, monsieur . . . Yesterday morning you were there when the magistrate asked me all those questions. . . . You asked me some yourself. And the little fellow who was the magistrate wrote it all down on paper. He came back in the afternoon to make me sign my statement. . . . Isn't that right?"

"Quite correct . . ."

"Well, now, you're asking me the same things . . . and I tell you it's not right. . . . Because, if I make any mistake, you'll think I've been telling you lies. . . . I'm not an educated man, monsieur. . . . I didn't hardly go to school. . . . Nor did Hubert. But we're both workers, and Anneke's a working woman, too."

"I'm only trying to check up. . . ."

"Check up on nothing . . . I was quietly in my boat, as you were at home . . . A man was thrown into the water, and I jumped into the punt to fish him out. . . . I'm not asking for a reward or for congratulations. . . . But that's no reason to come bothering me with questions. That's the way it seems to me, monsieur. . . ."

"We've found the two men who were in the red car."

Did Jef's brow really darken, or was it just an impression of Maigret's?

"Well, you've only got to ask them . . ."

"They declare that it was not midnight, but half past eleven, when they drove down onto the bank. . . ."

"Perhaps their watches were slow, eh?"

"We checked their evidence. . . . They went on to a café in Rue de Turenne and got there at twenty minutes to twelve. . . ."

Jef looked at his brother, who had glanced quickly at him.

"We might go and sit inside?"

The big cabin served both as kitchen and living room, and a stew was simmering on the white enamel stove. Madame van Houtte, who was nursing her baby, hurried into a bedroom, where the superintendent glimpsed a bed covered with a quilt.

"Sit down, won't you?"

Still hesitant, with apparent reluctance he opened the glass-fronted sideboard and took out a brown earthenware jug of gin and two thick-bottomed glasses.

Through the square windows they could see the trees along the bank, and occasionally the red roof of a villa. There was a longish silence, during which Jef remained standing, his glass in his hand. Finally he drank a mouthful, holding it for some time in his mouth before swallowing it.

"Is he dead?" he asked at last.

"No. He's recovered consciousness."

It was Maigret's turn, now, to remain silent. He looked round at the embroidered curtains on the windows, the brass containers holding green plants in pots, a photograph on the wall in a gilt frame, showing a stout middle-aged man in a sailor's sweater and cap.

This was the kind of figure one often saw on boats, thick-set and broad-shouldered, with a walrus mustache.

"Is that your father?"

"No, monsieur. It's Anneke's father."

"Was your father a bargeman, too?"

"My father was a longshoreman, monsieur, at Antwerp. . . . And that's not a job for a Christian, you know. . . ."

"That was why you became a bargeman?"

"I've been working on barges since I was thirteen, and nobody's ever had any complaints to make about me."

"Last night . . ."

Maigret thought he had disarmed him by these indirect questions, but the man shook his head.

"No, monsieur . . . It's not on . . . You've only got to look at that paper again."

"And what if I should discover that your answers were untrue?"

"Then you can do what you like. . . ."

"Did you see the two men from the car come out from under the Pont Marie?"

"Read the statement. . . ."

"They declare that they never went past your barge."

"People can say what they like, can't they?"

"They also assert that they saw nobody on the quay-side and that they only threw a dead dog into the Seine."

"It's not my fault if they say it was a dog."

The young woman came back without the child, which she must have put to bed. She spoke a few words in Flemish to her husband, who nodded, and she began to strain the soup.

The boat was slowing down. Maigret wondered if they had reached Mantes, but through the window he presently caught sight of a tug followed by three barges, slowly traveling upstream. They were passing under a bridge.

"Does the boat belong to you?"

"It's mine and Anneke's, yes. . . ."

"Your brother is not co-owner?"

"What's that mean?"

"He doesn't own part of it?"

"No, monsieur . . . The boat's mine and Anneke's."

"So your brother works for you?"

"Yes, monsieur . . ."

Maigret was getting used to his accent, to his repetitive "monsieur" and "n'est-ce-pas." It was clear from the young woman's expression that she understood only a few words of French and was wondering what the two men could possibly be saying.

"How long has he been doing so?"

"About a couple of years . . ."

"Before that, did he work on another boat? In France?"

"He worked like we do, sometimes in Belgium, sometimes in France. . . . It depends on the cargoes. . . ."

"Why did you send for him?"

"Because I needed somebody, vou see. . . . It's a big boat, you know. . . ."

"And before?"

"Before what?"

"Before you sent for your brother?"

Maigret was moving cautiously, choosing the most innocuous questions lest his interlocutor should jib again.

"I don't follow . . ."

"Was there somebody else to help you?"

"Sure . . ."

Before replying, he had glanced at his wife as though to make certain that she had not understood.

"Who was it?"

Jef filled the glasses in order to give himself time to think.

"It was me," he finally declared.

"You were the crew?"

"I was the mechanic."

"Who was the skipper?"

"I wonder if you've really got the right to ask me all these questions. A man's private life is his own business. . . . And I'm a Belgian, monsieur. . . ."

As he began to lose his temper, his accent become more marked.

"That's no way to behave, I must say. . . . My business doesn't concern anybody else, and just because I'm a Fleming isn't a reason to go meddle with my belongings. . . ."

Maigret took a few moments to understand the expression and could not restrain a smile.

"I might come back with an interpreter and question your wife."

"I won't have Anneke bothered. . . ."

"You may have to, if I bring a warrant from the magistrate. . . . I wonder now if it would not be simpler to take all three back to Paris. . . ."

"And then what would become of the boat? That you've no right to do, I'm sure. . . ."

"Why don't you just answer my questions?"

Van Houtte, with lowered head, glanced furtively at Maigret, like a schoolboy planning mischief.

"Because it's my own business. . . ."

So far, he was quite right. Maigret had no serious pretext for worrying him in this way. He was acting on intuition. He had been struck by the attitude of the bargeman when he went on board near Juziers.

Jef was not quite the same man that he had been in Paris. He had been surprised to see the superintendent on the riverbank and had reacted sharply. Since then he had remained suspicious and withdrawn, without that glint in the eyes, that touch of humor he had displayed on the Quai des Célestins.

"Well, am I to take you along?"

"You'll have to have a reason. We've got laws. . . ."

"The reason is that you refuse to answer ordinary routine questions. . . ."

The diesel was still chugging away, and Hubert's long legs could be glimpsed as he stood beside the tiller.

"Because you're trying to confuse me. . . ."

"I'm not trying to confuse you but to establish the truth. . . ."

"What truth?"

He seemed of two minds, now sure of his rights and now, on the contrary, obviously ill at ease.

"When did you buy this boat?"

"I didn't buy it."

"But yet it belongs to you?"

"Yes, monsieur, it belongs to me and it belongs to my wife. . . ."

"In other words, it was when you married her that you became owner of it. . . . Did the boat belong to her?"

"What's so odd about that? We got married quite legally, in front of the burgomaster and the priest. . . ."

"Until then her father had been skipper of the *Zwarte Zwaan*?"

"Yes, monsieur . . . It was old Willems."

"He had no other children?"

"No, monsieur . . ."

"What happened to his wife?"

"She'd been dead a year already. . . ."

"Were you working on the boat by then?"

"Yes, monsieur . . ."

"Since when?"

"Old Willems took me on when his wife died. . . . It was at Audenarde."

"Were you working on another boat at the time?"

"Yes, monsieur . . . the *Drie Gebrouders* . . ."

"Why did you change?"

"Because the *Drie Gebrouders* was an old barge that scarcely ever came to France and mostly carried coal. . . ."

"You dislike carrying coal?"

"It's dirty. . . ."

"So you came aboard this boat about three years ago. . . . How old was Anneke at that time?"

On hearing her name, she glanced at them with curiosity.

"Eighteen, *n'est-ce-pas?*"

"Her mother had just died. . . ."

"Yes, monsieur . . . At Audenarde, as I've already told you."

He was listening to the sound of the engine and looking at the bank; he went up to say a word to his brother, who slowed down to pass under a railway bridge.

Maigret patiently picked up his tangled skein, trying to follow a very slender thread.

"Until then, they had run the boat as a family. . . . When the mother died they needed somebody. . . . Is that right?"

"That's right . . ."

"You looked after the engine. . . ."

"The engine and all the rest . . . On board you've got to do a bit of everything. . . ."

"Did you fall in love with Anneke right away?"

"That's a personal matter, monsieur, *n'est-ce-pas?* That's my business and her business."

"When did you get married?"

"It'll be two years come next month. . . ."

"When did Willems die? Is that his portrait on the wall?"

"That's him."

"When did he die?"

"Six weeks before our wedding . . ."

More and more, Maigret had the feeling that his progress was discouragingly slow, and he summoned up all his patience, moving round in ever-narrowing circles so as not to scare the Fleming.

"Had the banns been published when Willems died?"

"In our country they publish the banns three weeks before the wedding. . . . I don't know what they do in France."

"But the marriage had been arranged?"

"Must have been, since we got married . . ."

"Would you put that question to your wife?"

"Why should I put a question like that to her?"

"Otherwise I shall be obliged to have an interpreter do so. . . ."

"Well . . ."

He was about to say, "You do that!"

And Maigret would have been most embarrassed. They were in the department of Seine-et-Oise now, and the superintendent was not entitled to carry on such an inquiry.

By chance, Van Houtte changed his mind and spoke to his wife in their own language. She blushed in surprise, looked at her husband, and then at their guest, saying something with a slight smile.

"Would you translate?"

"Well, she says, you see, that we'd loved each other for a long time. . . ."

"For nearly a year, by then?"

"Almost right away . . ."

"In other words, it began as soon as you came to live on board. . . ."

"What's wrong . . ."

Maigret interrupted. "What I'm wondering is whether Willems knew about it. . . ."

Jef did not answer.

"I suppose that, to begin with, in any event, like most other lovers, you kept out of his way?"

Once more the bargeman was staring out the window.

"We're nearly there now. . . . My brother needs me on deck."

Maigret followed him up, and there, in fact, were the wharfs of Mantes-la-Jolie, the bridge, and a dozen barges moored in the river port.

The engine had slowed down. When it reversed, a wash of great bubbles broke around the stern. There were people watching; there were other boats. A boy twelve years old caught hold of the mooring rope.

It was obvious that the presence of Maigret in his business suit and felt hat aroused some curiosity.

From one of the barges somebody hailed Jef in Flemish, and he replied in the same tongue, carefully maneuvering his boat meanwhile.

Inspector Neveu was standing on the quay, a cigarette between his lips, beside the little black car, and not far from an enormous pile of bricks.

"I hope you're going to leave us alone now? It's time

for us to eat. People like us get up at five in the morning."

"You haven't answered my question."

"Which question?"

"You haven't told me whether Willems was aware of your relations with his daughter."

"Did I marry her or didn't I?"

"You married her after he died."

"Was it my fault that he died?"

"Had he been ill for a long time?"

Once again they were standing in the stern of the boat, and Hubert was listening to them with a puzzled frown.

"He was never ill in his life, unless being drunk every night is an illness. . . ."

Maigret might have been mistaken, but it seemed to him that Hubert was surprised by the turn their talk had taken, and was watching his brother with a peculiar expression.

"Did he die of delirium tremens?"

"What's that?"

"The way drunkards usually end up . . . They have an attack which . . ."

"He didn't have any attack. . . . He was so tight that he fell . . ."

"In the water?"

Jef did not seem to welcome the presence of his brother, who was still listening.

"Into the water, yes . . ."

"Was it in France that this happened?"

He nodded again.

"In Paris?"

"Paris was where he used to drink most. . . ."

"Why?"

"Because he used to meet some woman, I don't know where, and they spent part of the night getting drunk together. . . ."

"Do you know the woman?"

"I don't know her name."

"Nor where she lives?"

"No."

"But you saw her with him?"

"I met them together and once I saw them go into a hotel. There's no point in telling Anneke. . . ."

"Doesn't she know how her father died?"

"She knows how he died, but she was never told about the woman."

"Would you recognize her?"

"Maybe . . . I'm not sure. . . ."

"Was she with him at the time of the accident?"

"I don't know. . . ."

"How did it happen?"

"I can't tell you, for I wasn't there."

"Where were you?"

"In my bunk . . ."

"And Anneke?"

"In her bunk . . ."

"What time was it?"

His answers came unwillingly, but they came none-theless.

"After two in the morning."

"Was it usual for Willems to come back so late?"

"In Paris, yes, on account of that woman . . ."

"What happened?"

"I've told you. He fell in."

"While he was crossing the gangway?"

"I suppose so."

"Was it in summer?"

"In December . . ."

"Did you hear a noise when he fell?"

"I heard something bumping against the hull."

"And cries?"

"He didn't call out."

"Did you hurry to help him?"

"Of course."

"Without bothering to get dressed?"

"I pulled on my trousers."

"Did Anneke hear, too?"

"Not immediately . . . She woke up when I went on deck."

"While you were going up, or after you were already there?"

There was something very like hatred in Jef's look.

"Ask her . . . If you think I can remember . . ."

"You saw Willems in the water?"

"I saw nothing at all. I could only hear something moving."

"Couldn't he swim?"

"He could swim. I suppose he wasn't able to. . . ."

"Did you jump into the punt, as you did on Monday night?"

"Yes, monsieur . . ."

"Did you succeed in pulling him out of the water?"

"Not for a good ten minutes, because each time I tried to catch hold of him he disappeared. . . ."

"Was Anneke standing on deck?"

"Yes, monsieur . . ."

"Was the man dead when you brought him out?"

"I didn't know as yet that he was dead. I know he was purple in the face, that's all. . . ."

"Did the doctor come? The police?"

"Yes, monsieur. Are you going to ask me any more questions?"

"Where did this take place?"

"In Paris, I told you."

"Whereabouts in Paris?"

"We had taken on some wine at Mâcon and we were unloading it on the Quai de la Rapée. . . ."

Maigret managed to betray no surprise, no satisfaction. He suddenly seemed to have become more good-humored, as though his nerves were relaxed.

"I think I've nearly done . . . Willems was drowned one night by the Quai de la Rapée, while you were asleep on board and his daughter was asleep, too. Is that correct?"

Jef blinked.

"About a month later you married Anneke. . . ."

"It wouldn't have been proper to live on the boat together without being married."

"At what point did you send for your brother?"

"Right away . . . Three or four days after . . ."

"After your marriage?"

"No. After the accident."

The sun had disappeared behind the rosy roofs, but a strangely unreal, disturbing light still lingered.

Hubert, standing motionless at the tiller, seemed to be brooding

"I suppose *you* don't know anything about it?"

119

"About what?"

"About what happened on Monday night?"

"I was out dancing in the Rue de Lappe. . . ."

"And about Willems's death?"

"I was in Belgium when I got the telegram. . . ."

"Well, is that all?" asked Jef van Houtte impatiently. "Are we going to be able to eat our soup?"

And Maigret replied unconcernedly, with the utmost calm:

"I'm afraid not."

This produced a shock. Hubert looked up sharply and stared, not at the superintendent but at his brother. As for Jef, he demanded with an even more aggressive look in his eyes:

"And will you tell me why I mayn't eat my soup?"

"Because I intend to take you back to Paris."

"You've no right to do that."

"In an hour's time I can procure a summons signed by the examining magistrate. . . ."

"And what for, may I ask?"

"So that we can carry on this interrogation somewhere else."

"I've said all that I had to say."

"And in order to bring you face to face with the tramp that you pulled out of the Seine on Monday night."

Jef turned to his brother as though appealing for help.

"Hubert, do you believe the superintendent has the right . . ."

But Hubert kept silent.

"Do you want to take me in your car?"

He had recognized it on the quayside, near to where Neveu was standing, and he pointed to it.

"And when shall I be allowed to come back to my boat?"

"Maybe tomorrow . . ."

"And if not tomorrow?"

"In that case, it's possible that you might never come back to it."

"What's that you're saying?"

He had clenched his fists and for a moment seemed about to rush at Maigret.

"And what about my wife? And my child? What's it all about, what are these stories you've made up? I'm going to tell my consul. . . ."

"You're entitled to do so. . . ."

"You're joking, aren't you?"

He still could not believe it.

"A man who's done nothing can't be arrested on his own boat. . . ."

"I'm not arresting you."

"What d'you think you're doing, then?"

"I'm going to take you to Paris to confront you with a witness who cannot travel."

"I don't even know the man, I don't. . . . I pulled him out of the water because he was calling for help. If I'd known . . ."

His wife emerged and put a question to him in Flemish. He replied volubly. She looked at the three men in turn; then she spoke again, and Maigret could have sworn she was advising her husband to go along with the superintendent.

"And where am I going to sleep?"

"You'll be given a bed at the Quai des Orfèvres."

"In jail?"

"No. At police headquarters . . ."

"Am I allowed to change my clothes?"

The superintendent gave permission, and Jef disappeared with his wife. Hubert, left face to face with Maigret, said nothing, staring blankly at the passers-by and the cars on the bank. Maigret said nothing, either, and he felt exhausted by that desultory interrogation, during which he had repeatedly been so disheartened that he believed he would never get anywhere.

Hubert broke the silence first, in a conciliatory tone.

"You mustn't mind him. He's hot-tempered, but he doesn't mean any harm."

"Was Willems aware of Jef's relations with his daughter?"

"On board a boat it's not easy to hide things. . . ."

"Do you think he approved of the marriage?"

"I wasn't there. . . ."

"And do you believe he fell into the water while crossing the gangway one night when he was drunk?"

"That often happens, you know. . . . A lot of boatmen die that way."

Downstairs an argument was going on in Flemish, and Anneke's voice had a pleading note whereas her husband's sounded angry. Could he yet again be threatening to refuse to go with the superintendent?

She must have won the day, for Jef eventually emerged on deck, his hair sleek and still damp. He was wearing a white shirt that showed off his tanned skin, a blue suit that was almost new, a striped tie and black shoes, as though he was going to Sunday Mass.

He spoke to his brother again in Flemish, without a look at Maigret, then left the boat and made his way to the black car, where he stood waiting.

The superintendent opened the door, while Neveu watched them both in astonishment.

"Where to, Chief?"

"Quai des Orfèvres."

They completed the journey in darkness, the headlights shining now on trees, now on village houses, finally on the gray streets of the outer suburbs.

Maigret did not utter a word but smoked his pipe in one corner. Jef van Houtte was equally mute, and Neveu, impressed by this unusual silence, wondered what could have happened.

He ventured to ask, "Any luck, Chief?"

Receiving no reply, he just kept on driving the car.

It was eight o'clock at night when they entered the courtyard of police headquarters. Only a few windows still showed lights, but old Joseph was there at his post.

In the inspectors' room, there were only three or four men, among them Lapointe, busy at his typewriter.

"Get them to send up some sandwiches and beer."

"For how many?"

"For two . . . No, three, for I might need you. Are you free?"

"Yes, Chief . . ."

Standing in the middle of Maigret's office the bargeman seemed even taller and thinner, and his features more strongly marked.

"You may sit down, Monsieur van Houtte. . . ."

Jef scowled at the word "monsieur," interpreting it as a sort of threat.

"They're going to bring us sandwiches. . . ."

"And when can I see the consul?"

"Tomorrow morning . . ."

Sitting at his desk, Maigret called his wife.

"I shan't be back for dinner. . . . No . . . I might have to stay here part of the night."

She must have been longing to ask him heaps of questions, but she confined herself to one, knowing her husband's interest in the vagrant.

"He's not dead?"

"No . . ."

She did not ask him if he had arrested anyone. Since he had telephoned from his office and was planning to stay there part of the night, that meant that a cross-examination was taking place, or was about to begin.

"Good night . . ."

He looked up at Jef in some annoyance.

"I asked you to sit down. . . ."

It worried him to see that tall figure motionless in the middle of the room.

"And suppose I don't want to sit down? I've a right to stand up, haven't I?"

Maigret merely heaved a sigh and sat waiting patiently for the beer and sandwiches to be brought up from the Brasserie Dauphine.

SEVEN

Such nights, which eight times out of ten ended with a confession, had in course of time acquired their own rules, their traditions, as it were, like stage plays that have been performed hundreds of times.

The inspectors on duty in the various departments had immediately understood what was happening, as had the waiter from the Brasserie Dauphine who brought up sandwiches and beer.

His bad temper, his ill-repressed anger did not prevent the Fleming from eating heartily and tossing off his first glass of beer in one long gulp, meanwhile watching Maigret out of the corner of his eye.

Deliberately, by way of defiance or protest, he ate in a disgusting way, munching noisily with his mouth open and spitting out a hard morsel of ham on to the floor as he might have spat it into the water.

The superintendent, seemingly calm and bland, ignored this provocative behavior and let the man pace to and fro about the room like a caged animal.

Had he been right? Had he been wrong? The most difficult thing in an investigation is to know at what point to play high. Now there are no established rules. It depends on no particular factor; it's a matter of intuition.

125

On certain occasions he had attacked without any solid evidence to go on and had succeeded in a few hours. At other times, on the contrary, with all the trumps in his hand and a dozen witnesses, it had taken him the whole night.

It was important, too, to find the right tone, which was different for each interlocutor, and this was what he was hunting for as he finished eating, with his eye still on the bargeman.

"Do you want any more sandwiches?"

"All I want is to go back to my boat and my little wife!"

He was bound, in the end, to get tired of walking round and round, and would sit down. It was useless trying to rush that sort of man; and the way to deal with him was probably by the "wheedling" method, starting gently, without accusing him; making him admit to one important inconsistency, then another, some trivial mistake, in order little by little to get him caught up in the wheels.

The two men were alone. Maigret had sent Lapointe on an errand.

"Listen to me, Van Houtte . . ."

"I've been listening to you for hours, haven't I?"

"If it's gone on so long, it's perhaps because you've not been answering me frankly."

"You're going to call me a liar, maybe?"

"I'm not accusing you of lying, but of not telling me everything. . . ."

"And suppose I were to begin asking *you* questions about your wife or your children. . . ."

126

"You had a difficult childhood. . . . Did your mother take good care of you?"

"So it's my mother's turn now, is it? I'll have you know that my mother died when I was only five. And she was a decent woman, a saintly woman, and if she's looking down at me from Heaven at this moment . . ."

Maigret kept a straight face.

"Did your father not remarry?"

"That's another matter. . . . My father drank too much."

"At what age did you begin to earn your living?"

"I worked on a barge when I was thirteen. I told you that. . . ."

"Have you other brothers besides Hubert? A sister?"

"I've got a sister. So what?"

"Nothing. We're becoming acquainted . . ."

"Well then, if we're to become acquainted, I ought to be putting questions to you, too. . . ."

"I should raise no objection."

"You say that because you're in your own office and you think yourself almighty . . ."

Maigret had known from the start that it would be a lengthy, difficult business, because Van Houtte was not intelligent. Invariably, it was stupid people that gave him the most trouble, because they stubbornly refuse to answer and have no hesitation about denying what they have asserted an hour before, without worrying when their contradictions are pointed out.

Often, with an intelligent suspect, one merely has to disclose the flaw in his line of argument, in his system, and before long everything collapses.

"I think I'm right in assuming that you're a good worker . . ."

A suspicious sideways glance.

"Sure, I've always worked hard."

"Some bosses must have taken an unfair advantage of your youth and willingness. . . . One day you met Louis Willems, who drank as your father used to. . . ."

Standing motionless in the middle of the room, Jef was watching him like an animal scenting danger but still uncertain how the attack will come.

"I'm convinced that but for Anneke you'd not have stayed on board the *Zwarte Zwaan*, but moved to another boat. . . ."

"Madame Willems was a decent woman, too. . . ."

"And she was not proud or domineering like her husband. . . ."

"Who told you he was proud?"

"Wasn't he?"

"He was the boss, and he wanted everyone to know it."

"I'd wager that Madame Willems, if she had lived, would not have been opposed to your marrying her daughter. . . ."

He might have been an idiot, but he had a wild creature's instinct, and this time Maigret had gone too fast.

"That's your story, isn't it? Well, can't I invent stories, too?"

"It's your story, such as I imagine it, though I may be mistaken."

"And it's my bad luck if I get stuck in jail because of your mistake. . . ."

"Let me finish. . . . You had a difficult childhood. . . . When you were still a boy you worked as hard as a man. Then you met Anneke, and she looked at you in a way you'd never been looked at before. . . . She considered you as a human being, not just as somebody who did all the chores on the boat and got all the abuse. Naturally you fell in love with her. No doubt her mother, if she'd been alive, would have encouraged your relations. . . ."

Phew! The man had sat down at last; true, he was only perching on the arm of a chair, but that was progress already.

"And what next? It's a good story, you know. . . ."

"Unfortunately Madame Willems was dead. You were alone on board the boat with her husband and Anneke. You were in contact with Anneke all day, and I bet Willems kept an eye on you. . . ."

"That's what you say. . . ."

"As the owner of a fine boat, he didn't want his daughter to marry a penniless fellow. . . . When he'd had a drink he turned rough and unpleasant."

Maigret had recovered his prudence and was observing Jef's eyes relentlessly.

"D'you think I'd let any man lay a hand on me?"

"I'm sure not. Only it wasn't on you that he laid a hand. . . . It was on his daughter. I wonder whether perhaps he didn't catch you together. . . ."

It was wiser to let a few moments elapse, and the silence hung heavy while the smoke rose gently from Maigret's pipe.

"You provided me with an interesting detail just now. . . . It was chiefly in Paris that Willems went out at night, because he met his woman friend and they got drunk together. . . .

"Elsewhere he drank on board the boat or in a pub near the quayside. Like all boatmen who, as you told me, get up before dawn, he must have gone early to bed. . . .

"In Paris you and Anneke had the opportunity to be alone together. . . ."

There was a sound of footsteps and voices from the next room. Lapointe half opened the door.

"Job's done, Chief . . ."

"Presently . . ."

And the "wheedling" went on in Maigret's smoke-filled office.

"It's possible that one night he may have come back earlier than usual and found you in one another's arms. . . . If that's what happened, he must certainly have flown into a rage. . . . And his rages must have been terrible. . . . He may have threatened to fling you out . . . and struck his daughter."

"That's your story," Jef repeated in an ironical tone.

"It's the story I should choose if I were in your shoes. For in that case Willems's death would have been almost an accident."

"It was an accident."

"I said almost. . . . I'm not even suggesting that you helped him fall into the water. He was drunk . . . walking unsteadily. Was it raining that night?"

"Yes."

"You see! So the plank was slippery. . . . What you did wrong was not to go to his rescue immediately. Unless it was something more serious, and you pushed him ... All this happened two years ago and the police report mentions an accident, not a murder."

"Well then? Why do you persist in blaming me for it?"

"I'm only trying to explain it. . . . Suppose, now, that somebody had seen you push Willems into the water. Somebody who was on the embankment, unseen by you . . . He could have told the police that you had waited on deck a longish time before jumping into the punt, in order to give your boss time to drown."

"And what about Anneke? Did she stand there watching without saying a word?"

"At two in the morning, she was probably asleep. In any case the man who saw you, and at that time used to sleep under the Pont de Bercy, said nothing to the police. Down-and-outs aren't keen on meddling in other people's business. . . . They don't look at things the way other people do, and they have their own ideas about justice.

"You were able to marry Anneke, and as you needed somebody with you to sail the boat, you sent for your brother from Belgium. . . . You had found happiness at last. You were your own boss now.

"Since then, you've passed through Paris several times, and I'll bet you've avoided mooring by the Pont de Bercy. . . ."

"No, monsieur! I've moored there at least three times."

"Because the Doc was no longer there. . . . Bums move around, too, and yours had settled underneath the Pont Marie.

"On Monday, he recognized the *Zwarte Zwaan.* . . . He recognized you. . . . I wonder . . ."

He appeared to be following out a fresh idea.

"You wonder what?"

"I wonder if on the Quai de la Rapée, when Willems was pulled out of the water, you didn't catch sight of him. . . . Yes, you must almost certainly have seen him. He came close but he said nothing. . . .

"On Monday, when he began prowling round near your boat, you realized that he might talk. . . . He may quite possibly have threatened to do so."

Maigret did not believe that. The Doc was not that sort. But for the time being his story required it.

"And then I threw him into the water, eh?"

"Let's say you jostled him. . . ."

Once again Jef was on his feet, calmer and more resolute than ever.

"No, monsieur! You'll never make me admit such a thing. It's not the truth."

"Then if I've been mistaken in any detail, tell me."

"I've told it all already. . . ."

"What?"

"It's been written down in black and white by the little man who came with the magistrate."

"You stated that toward midnight you heard a noise. . . ."

"If I said so, it's true."

"You added that two men, one of whom wore a light-colored raincoat, were just coming out from under the Pont Marie and hurrying toward a red car. . . ."

"It was red. . . ."

"They must have passed alongside your barge. . . ."

Van Houtte did not stir a muscle. Maigret went to the door and opened it.

"Come in, messieurs . . ."

Lapointe had gone to fetch the insurance agent and his stuttering friend from their homes. He had found them playing a three-handed game of *belote* with Madame Guillot, and they had followed him without demur. Guillot was wearing the same yellowish raincoat as on Monday night.

"Are these the two men who went off in the red car?"

"It's a different matter seeing people at night on a dark quayside and seeing them in an office. . . ."

"They answer to the description you gave. . . ."

Jef shook his head, still refusing to commit himself.

"They were, in fact, at the Port des Célestins that night. Monsieur Guillot, would you tell us what you did there?"

"We drove down the ramp. . . ."

"How far from the bridge was this ramp?"

"More than thirty yards."

"Did you stop the car just at the foot of the ramp?"

"Yes."

"And then?"

"We took the dog out of the trunk of the car."

"Was it heavy?"

"Nestor weighed more than I do. One hundred and fifty-five pounds two months ago, last time we weighed him on the butcher's scales . . ."

"Was there a barge beside the embankment?"

"Yes."

"Did you then both go toward the Pont Marie, carrying your burden?"

Hardoin had opened his mouth to protest, but fortunately his friend broke in first.

"Why should we have gone to the Pont Marie?"

"Because this gentleman asserts that you did."

"He saw us go toward the Pont Marie?"

"Not exactly. He saw you coming back from it."

The two men stared at one another.

"He can't have seen us walking alongside the barge, because we threw the dog into the river astern of it. . . . I was even afraid the sack might get caught in the rudder. . . . I waited a moment to make sure that the current was carrying him out into midstream."

"Do you hear, Jef?"

And Jef, quite untroubled, replied: "That's his story, isn't it? And you've told your story, too. . . . And perhaps there'll be still more stories. . . . It's none of my fault."

"What time was it, Monsieur Guillot?"

But Hardoin could not resign himself to playing a silent role, and began: "Half pa—pa—past ele—le—"

"Half past eleven," his friend interrupted. "The proof is that we were in the café in Rue de Turenne at twenty to twelve. . . ."

"Is your car a red one?"

"A red 403, yes . . ."

"Does the license plate include two nines?"

"7949 LF 75 . . . If you want to see the license . . ."

"Monsieur van Houtte, do you want to go down into the courtyard to identify the car?"

"I don't want anything except to go back to my wife."

"How do you explain these contradictions?"

"It's up to you to explain things. It's not my job."

"You know where you went wrong?"

"Yes. In pulling the man out of the water."

"That, to begin with . . . but you didn't do it on purpose."

"What d'you mean, I didn't do it on purpose? Was I walking in my sleep when I untied the punt and took the boat hook to try and . . ."

"You're forgetting that somebody else had heard the vagrant's shouts. Willems had not called out, probably because of shock on contact with the cold water. . . .

"In the case of the Doc, you took care to knock him out beforehand. You thought he was dead, or as good as dead, and that in any case he would be unable to resist the current and the eddies. . . .

"You were unpleasantly surprised when you heard him shouting for help. And you'd have left him to go on shouting if you had not heard another voice, that of the skipper of the *Poitou*. . . . He could see you standing on the deck of your barge. . . .

"Then you thought it would be clever to play the rescuer. . . ."

Jef merely shrugged his shoulders.

"When I told you a moment ago that you'd gone wrong, this is not what I was referring to. . . . I was thinking of your story. . . . For you chose to tell a story in order to avert any suspicion. And you worked it out elaborately."

The insurance agent and his friend, much impressed,

looked at the superintendent, and the bargeman, in turn, realizing at last that a man's life was at stake.

"At half past eleven you were not busy working at your engine, as you claimed, but you were at some spot from which you could see the embankment, either in the cabin or somewhere on deck. Otherwise you could not have seen the red car.

"You witnessed the dog being thrown into the water. . . . You remembered that when the police asked you what had happened.

"You felt sure the car would not be traced and you spoke of two men coming back from under the Pont Marie."

"I'm not stopping you talking, am I? They tell what stories they like and you can tell what stories you like."

Maigret went to the door again.

"Come in, Monsieur Goulet . . ."

This was the skipper of the *Poitou*, which was still unloading sand on the Quai des Célestins; he, too, had been brought in by Lapointe.

"What time was it when you heard someone calling out from the river?"

"About midnight."

"You can't be more specific?"

"No."

"It was later than half past eleven?"

"It must have been. When it was all over, I mean when we'd hoisted the body on the bank and the policeman had come, it was half past twelve. . . . I believe the officer noted the time in his book . . . and not more than half an hour had gone by since. . . ."

136

"What d'you say to that, Van Houtte?"

"Me? Nothing, see? He's telling a story. . . ."

"And the policeman?"

"The policeman's telling a story, too . . ."

By 10:00 P.M. the three witnesses had left, and a new tray of sandwiches and beer had been sent up from the Brasserie Dauphine. Maigret went into the next room and told Lapointe:

"It's your turn now. . . ."

"What am I to ask him?"

"Anything you like . . ."

This was a routine practice. Sometimes three or four of them would take it in relays during the night, putting roughly the same questions in a fresh way in order gradually to wear down the suspect's resistance.

"Hullo! Put me through to my wife, would you?"

Madame Maigret had not yet gone to bed.

"You'd better not wait up for me."

"You sound tired. . . . Is it being difficult?"

She had sensed discouragement in his voice.

"He'll go on denying to the end, without giving us the least handle. . . . He's the finest specimen of an obstinate idiot that I've ever been confronted with. . . ."

"And the Doc?"

"I'm going to inquire about him."

He next rang the Hôtel Dieu and spoke to the nurse on night duty in the surgical ward.

"He's asleep. No, he's in no pain. . . . The doctor came to see him after dinner and considers him to be out of danger."

"Has he spoken?"

"Before going to sleep he asked me for a drink. . . ."

"He's said nothing else?"

"No. He took his sedative and closed his eyes."

Maigret paced up and down the passage for half an hour, giving Lapointe his opportunity; he could hear the murmur of the inspector's voice behind the closed door. Then he went back into his office, to find Jef van Houtte seated on a chair at last, with his big hands folded on his knees.

The inspector's expression told him clearly enough that he had got no results, while there was a look of mockery on the face of the bargeman.

"Is it going on much longer?" he inquired, watching Maigret resume his seat. "Don't forget that you promised me to send for the consul. I shall tell him everything you've done, and it'll be in all the Belgian newspapers."

"Listen to me, Van Houtte . . ."

"I've been listening to you for hours, and you've kept on repeating the same thing."

He pointed to Lapointe: "So has he. . . . Are there some more of them, behind that door, coming to ask me questions?"

"Perhaps there are . . ."

"I shall give them the same answers."

"You've contradicted yourself several times."

"And what if I did contradict myself? Wouldn't you contradict yourself if you were in my shoes?"

"You've heard the witnesses. . . ."

"The witnesses say one thing. . . . I say another. . . . That doesn't mean that it's me that's lying. I've worked hard all my life. Ask any bargeman what he thinks of

Jef van Houtte. Not one of them'll have a thing to say against me."

And Maigret started again from the beginning, determined to keep on trying, remembering one case where the man sitting opposite him, as tough as the Fleming, had suddenly yielded after sixteen hours, just as the superintendent had been about to give up.

It was one of the most exhausting nights he had ever spent. Twice he withdrew into the next room and let Lapointe take over. By the end there were no more sandwiches, no more beer, and they felt as if the three of them were alone, like ghosts, in the deserted buildings of police headquarters, where cleaning women had begun sweeping the corridors.

"It's impossible that you should have seen the two men walking alongside the barge. . . ."

"The difference between us is that I was there and you weren't. . . ."

"You heard what they said. . . ."

"Anyone can say anything. . . ."

"Note that I'm not accusing you of premeditation . . ."

"What does that mean?"

"I'm not saying that you knew beforehand that you were going to kill him."

"Who? Willems or the fellow I pulled out of the water? Because by now there are two of them, aren't there? And by tomorrow there may be three, or four, or five. It's easy enough for you to add some more."

By three o'clock Maigret, exhausted, decided to call a halt. For once it was he, and not his interlocutor, who had had enough of it. He got up.

"That'll do for today," he muttered.

"Can I go back to my wife, then?"

"Not yet . . ."

"Are you going to make me spend the night in jail?"

"You can go to bed here, in a room where there's a camp bed. . . ."

Lapointe took him there. Maigret, meanwhile, left police headquarters and walked, his hands in his pockets, through the deserted streets. It was only at Châtelet that he found a taxi.

He entered the bedroom noiselessly. Madame Maigret stirred in her bed and muttered sleepily, "Is that you?"

As though it could have been anyone else!

"What time is it?"

"Four o'clock . . ."

"Has he confessed?"

"No."

"You believe it's him?"

"I'm morally convinced of it. . . ."

"Have you had to let him go?"

"Not yet . . ."

"Wouldn't you like me to get you something to eat?"

He was not hungry, but he poured himself a drink before going to bed, which did not prevent him from lying awake for a good half-hour more.

He would not forget that Belgian boatman in a hurry!

EIGHT

Torrence went along with them that morning, for Lapointe had spent the night at headquarters. Maigret had had a longish telephone conversation beforehand with Dr. Magnin.

"I'm convinced that he has been fully conscious since yesterday evening," the doctor had declared. "I must just ask you not to tire him. Don't forget that he's had a severe shock, and it'll take him some weeks to recover from it completely."

The three of them walked along the embankment in the sunshine, Van Houtte between the superintendent and Torrence, and they might well have been mistaken for strollers enjoying a fine spring morning.

Van Houtte had not shaved, for lack of a razor, and the fair bristles on his face glistened in the sunlight.

Opposite the Palais de Justice they had stopped in a bar to drink coffee and eat *croissants*. The Fleming had devoured seven with the utmost calm.

He must have thought they were taking him to the Pont Marie for some sort of reconstruction and was surprised at being led into the gray courtyard of the Hôtel Dieu and then into the hospital corridors.

Although he gave a slight frown, he seemed unperturbed.

"May we go in?" Maigret asked the ward sister.

She scrutinized his companion with some curiosity and eventually shrugged her shoulders. It was beyond her; she gave up trying to understand.

This, the superintendent thought, was his last chance. He led the way into the ward, where as on the previous day the patients stared at him; Jef followed, partially concealed by Maigret, while Torrence brought up the rear.

The Doc watched him coming without apparent curiosity, and when he noticed the bargeman his attitude did not change.

As for Jef, he remained as unconcerned as he had been during the night. With dangling arms and an expression of indifference on his face, he surveyed the unfamiliar scene of a hospital ward.

The hoped-for shock did not occur.

"Come forward, Jef . . ."

"What have I got to do now?"

"Come here . . ."

"All right . . . What next?"

"Do you recognize him?"

"I suppose he's the chap that was in the water, isn't he? Only that night he had a beard. . . ."

"You recognize him all the same?"

"I think so . . ."

"And you, Monsieur Keller?"

Maigret almost held his breath, and kept his eyes fixed on the vagrant, who was gazing at him and who, slowly, made up his mind to look at the bargeman.

"Do you recognize him?"

Did Keller hesitate? The superintendent could have sworn to it. There was a long, expectant pause until the doctor from Mulhouse turned his gaze on Maigret again without any sign of emotion.

"Do you recognize him?"

He had to control himself, suddenly feeling an almost furious resentment against the man who, as he now knew, had decided to say nothing.

The proof was that the ghost of a smile flitted over the Doc's face and a mischievous gleam came into his eyes.

His lips parted and he muttered, "No."

"This is one of the two boatmen who pulled you out of the Seine."

"Thank you," whispered a barely audible voice.

"And it's also he, I'm practically certain, who gave you a knock on the head before throwing you into the water. . . ."

Silence. The Doc remained quite still, only his eyes showing any sign of life.

"Do you still not recognize him?"

What made the scene particularly impressive was that everything was said in hushed tones, while two rows of patients, lying in bed, watched and listened intently.

"Aren't you going to say anything?"

Keller still did not move.

"And yet you know why he attacked you. . . ."

The man's gaze betrayed a certain curiosity. He seemed surprised that Maigret had found out so much.

"It goes back to two years ago, when you were still living under the Pont de Bercy. . . . One night . . . can you hear me?"

143

He nodded.

"One night in December you witnessed a scene in which this man was involved. . . ."

Keller seemed, once again, to be wondering what decision to take.

"Another man, the skipper of the barge close to which you were lying, was pushed into the river. . . . And *he* did not survive."

There was still the same silence, and finally a look of complete indifference came over the injured man's face.

"Isn't that true? On seeing you again on Monday on the Quai des Célestins, the murderer was afraid of your speaking. . . ."

The head moved slightly, with an effort, just enough to enable Keller to catch sight of Jef van Houtte.

There was no hatred or resentment in his gaze, nothing but a certain curiosity.

Maigret realized that he would extract nothing further from the vagrant, and when the ward sister came to tell them they had stayed long enough, he did not protest.

In the corridor, the bargeman held his head high.

"You're none the wiser, are you?"

He was quite right. It was he who had won the game.

"I can make up stories, too," he remarked triumphantly.

And Maigret could not resist muttering between his teeth:

"To hell with you!"

While Jef waited at police headquarters with Torrence, Maigret spent nearly two hours in Judge Dantziger's chambers. The latter had called Deputy Public Prosecutor Parrain and asked him to join them, and the superintendent told his story from beginning to end, down to the smallest detail.

The magistrate made notes in pencil, and when the story was ended he sighed:

"In a word, we've not a single proof against him."

"No proof, no . . ."

"Apart from the question of the times which don't tally . . . Any good lawyer would tear that argument to shreds."

"I know . . ."

"Have you still any hope of getting a confession?"

"None at all," admitted the superintendent.

"Will the vagrant persist in keeping silent?"

"I'm convinced of it."

"What reason can you suggest for his attitude?"

That was harder to explain, particularly to people who were unacquainted with that small social group that lives under bridges.

"Yes, what reason?" put in the deputy public prosecutor. "After all, it was nearly the end of him. . . . In my opinion, he ought to . . ."

In the opinion of a deputy public prosecutor, of course, who lived in a flat in Passy with his wife and children, held weekly bridge parties, and was concerned with his own promotion and the scale of salaries.

But not in the opinion of a down-and-out.

"There's such a thing as justice, after all. . . ."

Yes, indeed. But, in fact, people who were not afraid of sleeping under bridges in midwinter, wrapped in old newspapers to keep themselves warm, were not interested in that sort of justice.

"Can you understand, yourself?"

Maigret was reluctant to say yes, for they would certainly have looked askance at him.

"You see, he doesn't think that a trial in the Assize Court, or counsels' speeches, or juries' decisions, or prison are terribly important things."

What would these two have said if he had told them how he had slipped that marble into the injured man's hand? And indeed if he had told them that Keller, sometime doctor, whose wife lived on the Ile Saint-Louis and whose daughter had married an important manufacturer of pharmaceutical products kept glass marbles in his pocket like a ten-year-old schoolboy?

"Is he still asking to see his consul?"

They were talking about Jef now.

And the magistrate, after a glance at the deputy public prosecutor, muttered with some hesitation:

"In the present state of the inquiry, I don't think I can sign a warrant for his arrest. From what you tell me, there would be no point in my having a turn at questioning him."

It was certainly unlikely that the magistrate would succeed where Maigret had failed.

"Well, then?"

Well, then, as Maigret had already known when he got there, the game was lost. There was nothing for it but to release Van Houtte, who might perhaps demand an apology.

"I'm sorry, Maigret. But as things now stand . . ."

"I know . . ."

It was always a difficult moment to live through. This was not the first time it had happened to him—and always with half-wits.

"I apologize, gentlemen," he muttered as he left them.

Back in his office, a little later, he had to say the same thing:

"I apologize, Monsieur van Houtte . . . That's to say, I apologize formally. . . . I'll have you know, however, that I've not changed my mind, that I'm still convinced that you killed your skipper, Louis Willems, and that you did all you could to get rid of the tramp, who was an awkward witness. . . .

"Having said this, I'll add that there's nothing to prevent you from returning to your barge and getting back to your wife and child. . . . Good-bye, Monsieur van Houtte. . . ."

What happened next, however, was that the bargeman made no protest, but merely looked at the superintendent in some surprise, and as he stood in the doorway stretched out his long arm and offered his hand, mumbling:

"Anyone can make a mistake, *n'est-ce-pas?*"

Maigret avoided looking at the hand, and five minutes later he had immersed himself frenziedly in current problems.

During the weeks that followed, an arduous series of checks were carried out both in the neighborhood of the Quai de Bercy and in that of the Pont Marie, and numbers of people were questioned, while the Belgian police sent reports that were added, all in vain, to other reports.

As for the superintendent, for three months he was often to be seen hanging about near the Quai des Célestins, with his pipe between his teeth and his hands in his pockets, as if he had nothing better to do. The Doc had finally been discharged from hospital. He had gone back to his nook under the bridge, and his belongings had been restored to him.

Sometimes Maigret would stop beside him, as though by chance. Their conversation was always brief.

"You all right?"

"I'm all right. . . ."

"None the worse for your injury?"

"Just a touch of dizziness from time to time . . ."

Although they avoided talking about the matter, Keller knew quite well what Maigret was after and Maigret knew that Keller knew. It had become a sort of game they played together.

A little game that went on until one morning in the full heat of summer, when the superintendent halted beside the Doc, who was eating a chunk of bread and drinking some red wine.

"You all right?"

"I'm all right!"

Had François Keller decided that his interlocutor had waited long enough? He was watching a barge moored nearby, a Belgian barge which was not the *Zwarte Zwaan*, but which looked like it.

"Those people have a good life," he commented.

And pointing to two fair-haired children playing on the deck, he added:

"Particularly those . . ."

Maigret looked him in the eyes, gravely, with a presentiment that there was something more to come.

"Life's not easy for anyone," the vagrant went on.

"Nor is death . . ."

"What's impossible is to pass judgment."

They understood one another.

"Thank you," murmured the superintendent, who knew the truth at last.

"For nothing . . . I've said nothing. . . ."

And the Doc added, like the Fleming, *"N'est-ce-pas?"*

And indeed he had said nothing. He refused to pass judgment. He would not give evidence.

Nevertheless, Maigret felt able to announce to his wife, casually, while they were having lunch:

"You remember the barge and the vagrant?"

"Yes. Anything new?"

"I wasn't mistaken. . . ."

"Have you arrested the man, then?"

He shook his head.

"No! Unless he does something rash, which would surprise me in his case; he'll never be arrested."

"Has the Doc spoken to you?"

"In a sort of way, yes . . ."

With his eyes, rather than with words. They had understood one another, and Maigret smiled on remembering the sort of understanding that had been established between them, for a brief moment, under the Pont Marie.

Noland
May 2, 1962